THE CALL

by Wendy Ulmer

illustrations by Sandra Salsbury

To Karson,

Be a good friend!

wendy R ulmer

2017

wooly moon books Maine • USA

wooly moon books
PO Box 274
Woolwich, ME 04579

www.wendyulmer.com
woolymoon@gmail.com
Printed and bound in the United States of America
First Edition
10 9 8 7 6 5 4 3 2 1
LCCN on file
ISBN 978-0-692-87032-7

This book was expertly produced by Book Bridge Press.
www.bookbridgepress.com

For *The Mustard Seed Bookstore,*
Bath, Maine, for providing me
a writing home
full of support and love

With thanks to Aimee, Lois, Helga, Eric, Darrin,
and AJ—the best book team ever!

And special thanks to Susan,
who always believed...
—W. U.

For Jacob
—S. S.

TABLE OF CONTENTS

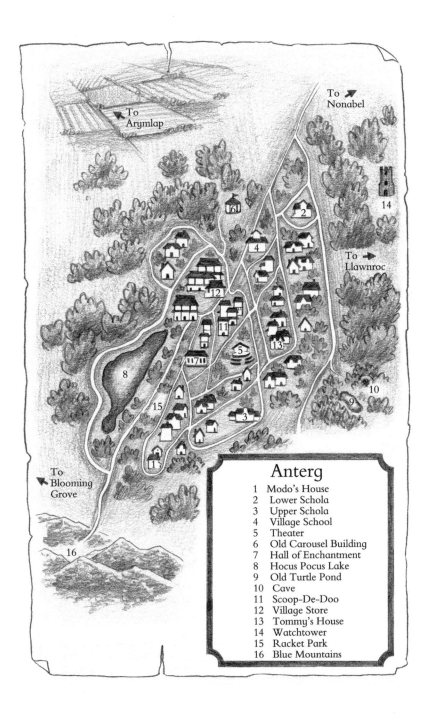

Anterg

1 Modo's House
2 Lower Schola
3 Upper Schola
4 Village School
5 Theater
6 Old Carousel Building
7 Hall of Enchantment
8 Hocus Pocus Lake
9 Old Turtle Pond
10 Cave
11 Scoop-De-Doo
12 Village Store
13 Tommy's House
14 Watchtower
15 Racket Park
16 Blue Mountains

To
Arymlap

To
Nonabel

To
Llawnroc

To
Blooming
Grove

LOWER SCHOLA

What if I'm not a magick?
Gavin will never let me forget it!
—MODO JOURNAL ENTRY

Modo sat at the kitchen table staring at his pancakes. The house was quiet except for the ticking of the old banjo clock and the chickadees calling in the trees outside. A soft breeze blew the kitchen curtains away from the windowsill, like sails on a boat filling with the wind. A single shaft of sunlight fell through the screen door onto the wooden floor and across the table, landing on Modo's small leather journal. The imprint of oak leaves and acorns on its cover seemed to almost glow in the sunlight. Modo touched the sliver of moon in the top right corner—the moon that identified him as the child of a magick.

The sound of feet pounding down the narrow wooden stairs from the second floor jarred Modo from his thoughts.

"Hey, little brother," Gavin exclaimed as he slid into the seat next to Modo, disturbing Finkle, their mother's cat.

"You better eat up; you'll need your strength today." Gavin laid his leather journal on the table next to Modo's wooden flute, a gift from his grandmother. Pushing his glasses up, Modo looked at the three crescent moons on Gavin's journal. Would his book ever look like that? Only if he got into Lower Schola. If he didn't, the sliver of the moon would become the star of a natural.

"Don't look so worried," Gavin said. His green eyes twinkled. "After you finish off the two trolls, it's all downhill." He grinned as he stuffed his lunch into his pack and slid his journal into his back pocket.

"Don't scare your brother," Mother called from the hall. "Let's go, Modo; we don't want to be late."

Modo followed Gavin out the front door and watched as he raced across the porch, tapping the back of each rocker so they all moved like a wave in front of the house. Jumping off the porch, Gavin ran ahead down the sun-sprinkled path to join his friends. They were all starting their fourth year at Lower Schola and would soon take tests for Upper Schola. Having magicks for parents didn't guarantee you would also be a magick. No one knew for sure if he or she were one until they took the test for Lower Schola. Sometimes when Modo played his flute, the air seemed to shimmer, like it was alive. Modo wasn't sure if that was magick, but today he would leave his test with either a crescent moon on his journal or a new natural star.

Modo lived in the village of Anterg, at the base of the Blue Mountains. There was a mystic stillness to the village, a stillness noticed by visitors and treasured

by the villagers. In the evening, neighbors settled into rocking chairs on large covered porches, their houses snuggled up next to each other. Spiderwebs decorated the spindled posts and corners of the porches along the moss-covered walkways. As daylight faded, small colored lanterns glowed on the porches, shining like tiny jewels in the coming darkness. There was the heavy scent of deep pine, and the rooftops of the cottages wore pale green lichen cloaks against the evening cool. The plants and animals of Anterg were part of the community, a community where naturals and magicks lived together in harmony with each other and nature.

Dry leaves crackled underfoot as Modo walked with his mother down the narrow pathway between the cottages. Scattered along the path and among the cottages, pines, maples, and oaks shook their leaves in welcome as Modo walked beneath them. Sitting in a tall pine, Father's crow, Mercedes, watched over the walkers.

"Look," said Modo as they walked the shadowy path. "There seem to be more Faerie rings today than usual." Wispy circles of white cottony webs dotted the dry leaves under the trees.

"You're right," Mom agreed. "They're even on the grassy lawn around the school!"

Lower Schola sat at the top of a small hill next to a tree-lined road that circled back to the main road. Several teachers and Principal Winkleberry lived in cottages along the curve. After climbing the stairs up to the front door, Modo found himself on a wide, covered porch with round white columns. Large shrubs and bushes closed in around the foundation of the school.

Opening the heavy wooden door, Modo and his mom stepped into a center hallway lined with knotty-pine walls and worn, flowered carpets scattered on the wide board floor. To the right was a door with a sign that said: "Lower Schola—come on in!"

They signed in with the secretary and took seats in hard wooden chairs. There were other young boys and girls there, some biting their nails or jiggling their feet. One by one, the children went into the principal's office. One by one they came out, either crying or waving their journals in the air.

"Modo Malarkey, please."

THE TEST

Principal Winkleberry sat behind an enormous desk in his office, which was filled with yellow warmth from the sunlight in the window. Principal Winkleberry was quite round, with full red cheeks resting over his polka-dot bow tie. A silver dragon, appearing to be perched on his chest, hung from a black leather cord around his neck. On the wall behind his desk, a watercolor of trees hung a bit crookedly, and the faint smell of cinnamon and carnations hung in the air. In the corner was a wooden music stand with a single sheet of music on it, "The Anthem of Anterg." An instrument case sat on the floor next to the stand.

He always liked testing day for the new students. Their eager faces were wonderful to see, but, of course, there were always a few disappointments. The door opened and a young boy with tight dark curls and large green eyes behind blue-rimmed glasses stood in the doorway. But the boy wasn't looking at him; he was staring at the large green egg snuggled up in a nest of blue cloth.

"Relax, Modo," Principal Winkleberry said. "Nothing in this test will hurt you; it will only take a moment. I imagine your brother, Gavin, tried to scare you. But that's what big brothers do, don't they?"

"Yes, sir," Modo whispered. The boy looked scared, almost like he wanted to turn and run.

"It's a simple test, Modo. I want you to look at this large egg. When you're ready, I want you to point at the egg and say your true special magick word. If you are a magick, the egg will crack open and inside will be a small figurine of your magical animal companion. If nothing happens, well, then you will not be attending Lower Schola. Whenever you're ready."

Principal Winkleberry sat quietly watching as panic crossed the boy's face and shivered through his little body. He could hear the boy whispering, *magick word, animal companion, Gavin…*

"Anytime, Modo," Principal Winkleberry said with a smile, adjusting the bow tie peeking out under his puffy chin.

The room darkened as a cloud moved over the sun. Suddenly, pushing up his glasses, the boy took a deep breath, pointed his finger at the egg, screwed his large green eyes shut, and then "Binga" flew out of his mouth.

Modo stood in front of the desk, not moving, and though his eyes remained closed, a look of amazement spread across his face. "Binga?" he whispered. "Where did that come from?"

Principal Winkleberry didn't move or breathe, but sat with his eyes glued on the egg. There was a rushing in his ears as his heart beat faster, and he suddenly gasped for air. Modo opened his eyes at the sound and stared at the desk.

"Unbelievable!" Principal Winkleberry half whispered, forgetting about Modo as the smell of cinnamon and carnations grew stronger.

There was no figurine in the egg, though the egg was indeed broken in half. Sitting in the broken shell, like a very small child, was a baby brown dragon, his tiny front claws grabbing his toes, his big ears laying against his scaly head, and his large black eyes looking up at Modo.

"Modo," said Principal Winkleberry, finally remembering he wasn't alone, "welcome to Lower Schola!"

Modo stood and stared—he couldn't take his eyes off the baby dragon. Principal Winkleberry knew how he felt. He remembered.

"How…how did it get here?" Modo whispered.

"Well," said Principal Winkleberry, "dragons choose their magicks, and this little one has chosen you!"

"What do I do with him?" Modo asked, his eyes still glued on the little creature squirming around, his tiny claws *scritch scritching* on the egg shell. Principal Winkleberry reached out, stroked the little dragon's head, and then moved his hand to the dragon pendant around his neck. It was so long ago for him, but it felt like it was just yesterday.

"Sir?" Modo asked.

"Oh, yes. Well, for now you must keep him safe and well fed. I'm afraid he will eat quite a bit."

"Maybe this is a mistake," Modo declared. "Why would a dragon want me?"

Principal Winkleberry smiled. "I'm sure it's not a mistake, Modo. Your family will help you care for him, but remember, he is *your* responsibility."

Modo leaned in and looked directly into the dragon's black eyes. The little dragon stopped moving, looked directly into Modo's green eyes, and squeaked, "Eboo, Eboo." Modo jumped back, falling into a chair.

Principal Winkleberry chuckled, and then became quite serious. *Dreyken must still be alive!*

"Sir?" Modo asked again. Principal Winkleberry looked up.

"Sir, did you have a dragon?"

"Actually," Principal Winkleberry replied, "I did. His name is Dreyken. He has been the leader of the dragons in Blooming Valley for a very long time." Principal Winkleberry paused and then continued, "But now there are some things you must know. Everyone who enters Lower Schola must promise to never tell anyone about their test or their individual magick word. You risk losing your magick if you share this information."

"Oh," Modo said. "That's why Gavin wouldn't tell me anything."

"Yes," the principal said. "Gavin did a good job. Keeping a secret is hard, especially from a brother."

Modo sat quietly for a moment, still looking at the dragon.

"I promise, sir," he said.

"There is one more thing, Modo," Principal Winkleberry said, now clutching the dragon pendant in his hand. "The dragon is unexpected. Dreyken was the last one in Anterg, almost 100 years ago. When a dragon arrives, it usually means there is some danger or threat developing. Until we know why he has come, he, too, must be kept secret."

Modo looked up and stared at the principal.

"Keep a dragon a secret? How am I going to do that? He's going to get big and he'll fly and he'll eat a lot and... and...and..."

"Easy, Modo," Principal Winkleberry said. "For a few weeks, it will be like having a regular pet. Hopefully, we will know more by then and we can figure out the next step. But for now, we don't want to cause any undue concern. Now, I'm going to speak with your mother, and when you're ready, come on out. You can wrap him in the blue cloth."

"Thank you, sir. But, how will I know his name?"

"He just told you. The first word uttered by a dragon is his name."

Principal Winkleberry watched quietly as Modo picked up the little creature and gently wrapped him in the blue cloth.

Modo smiled. "Hello, Eboo. My name is Modo, and I'm a magick!"

Closing the door behind him, Principal Winkleberry stood a moment in the outer office. Although he felt happy for Modo, he was filled with sadness.

BROTHERS

I can't believe this, I won't believe this!
Not my brother!!!
—GAVIN JOURNAL ENTRY

Modo sat on his bed paging through his schoolbooks. Glancing up, he caught sight of himself in the mirror on the opposite wall over his dresser. His dark curly hair was still in tight corkscrews against his head, his eyes were still green behind his blue-rimmed glasses, his ears were still too big. He didn't look any different than he did this morning, but everything felt different. He felt different. Next to the bed, sitting quietly in a dog crate, Eboo looked up at him with large black eyes.

Modo turned back to the books on his lap. There were the usual math, reading, and science books like his natural friend Tommy studied. But he also had the *Beginner's Guide to the World of Magicks.* Principal Winkleberry, however, had given him the book that was the most interesting. *What to Do When a Dragon Chooses You* was supposed to help him learn how to take care of Eboo. But no book could tell him how to deal with an angry brother.

After school, Gavin was excited when he heard that Modo was in Lower Schola.

"Now I don't have to be embarrassed that I have a natural for a brother!" Gavin smiled and high-fived Modo. Mother glared at Gavin as she put a plate of cookies on the kitchen table. "Just kidding. When you're older and know some magic, we can play Magick Mania. It's a blast! Isn't it, Dad?"

"Yes," Father said. "It's great fun. Modo, did you tell Gavin about your test?"

"What's there to tell?" Gavin asked, grabbing a cookie from the plate. "He passed!"

"Well," Modo said. "Something unexpected happened. I was chosen by my animal companion."

"What?" Gavin shouted, clenching his fist, crumbling the cookie. "We don't get chosen by our animals until we've proven ourselves in Upper Schola!"

All magicks look forward to the day their magick animal companion appears. They know from their test for Lower Schola what their animal will be, but only the magick animal can choose them. Most magicks are chosen before the end of Upper Schola, though some are older before they are chosen.

Gavin's face turned bright red as he paced the creaky kitchen floor. Stopping in front of Modo, he said, "Maybe there's something wrong with your animal, maybe it's messed up somehow."

"There's nothing wrong with Modo's dragon," Father said, picking up a glass of lemonade from the table.

"A dragon?" Gavin stopped abruptly. "You've got to be kidding."

Every kid—magick and natural—knew it had been almost 100 years since the last dragon flew out of Anterg. Dragons were of history, legend, and storybooks, not part of their lives.

"Gavin," Modo said, "he's really cool. Come up and see him."

"He's in your bedroom?" Gavin asked. "Make sure you keep him out of my room. I don't need some stupid dragon stinking up my space!"

"Gavin, this means changes for all of us," Mother said. "We can't speak of the dragon outside the house, not even to other magicks. Until we know why Modo was chosen, why the dragon is here, we *must* keep Eboo a secret."

"Eboo?" Gavin sneered. "That's a weird name."

"Do you understand, Gavin? This is important, and we must all keep the secret."

"I understand," Gavin grumbled as he headed out the screen door, letting it slam behind him, "but it doesn't mean I have to like it."

Father smiled at Modo. "Maybe you should go check on Eboo." Modo grabbed a cookie and headed up the narrow wooden stairs to his bedroom.

Three days went by and Gavin still wouldn't talk to Modo. He wouldn't walk to school with him or sit by him at the dinner table. Modo missed his brother. He needed him. Eboo was often hungry and it was hard to carry enough food up to his room by himself. Although Eboo and Modo were both young, the book said Eboo would grow much faster than his magick. Most magicks were almost grown when their animals chose them. But Modo was still a boy and had a lot of growing to do. Eboo was a little dragon and he had a lot of growing to do too. He needed food, lots and lots of food!

"*Chow now?*" Eboo squeaked.

"Soon," Modo answered. "Do you like peanut butter?"

"*Peanut butter in the gutter. Time to eat, Eboo wants meat!*"

Modo sighed. "Okay, I'll see what I can find." He headed down the narrow wooden stairs to the kitchen, hoping there was some kind of meat in the cold cupboard. Then he would look for a part in the book that might explain why Eboo talked in rhymes.

THE BOOK

Could Eboo really be more than an ordinary dragon?
That's crazy. There's nothing ordinary about any dragon!
—MODO JOURNAL ENTRY

Modo returned to his room with three pork chops, half a chicken, and two dozen eggs. At this rate, he would have to stop eating so they could afford to feed Eboo. Modo was sure Mother would be angry when she saw him carry all the food upstairs, but she just smiled and rushed ahead to open the bedroom door for him. Finkle slipped through the door first and curled up on top of Eboo's crate.

Eboo flapped his wings and hopped around when he saw Modo.

"*Modo brings meat for Eboo to eat. Eboo grows stronger, time to fly not much longer!*"

"Enjoy your meat, Eboo. Dad's making a bridle for you to wear when you fly. I showed it to him in the book

Principal Winkleberry gave me; maybe this weekend we can try it. I bet Mercedes will help."

With Finkle softly purring and Eboo crunching and slurping in the background, Modo opened the book and looked at the Table of Contents. There were the expected sections: What to Feed Your Dragon, First Aid for Dragons, Trouble-shooting Flying Problems.

"This might be it," Modo muttered, pushing up his glasses as Eboo noisily sucked down eggs. "Special Characteristics and What They Mean, page 167." Modo looked through the book until he found the page. In large letters at the top of the chapter was written: BE ADVISED: NOT ALL DRAGONS HAVE THESE CHARACTERISTICS OR HABITS AND NO DRAGON HAS ALL OF THEM! There were different headings for each characteristic, followed by a few sentences explaining the dragon's behavior.

Modo read:

> *Humming: a dragon hums when he is especially*
> *   pleased and content. Be happy when your*
> *   dragon hums.*
> *Steaming nostrils: some dragons have a*
> *   minor nose defect and steam occasionally*
> *   leaks out unintentionally. The dragon cannot*
> *   control this, so it is wise to never bend over in*
> *   front of your dragon.*

Persistent sneezing with flying sparks: this condition is usually a result of allergies. Change your dragon's food or where he sleeps. Difficult cases may sometimes need a Pepper Purging Potion; see your local Pharmacy Wizard for help. Keep a fire extinguisher nearby.

Scale dropping: *this is often a result of a blocked or missing oil gland. As dragons are extremely sensitive about having their oil glands examined, the safest treatment is to feed your dragon ten cod fish a week to substitute for the missing natural oil.*

The list continued until near the bottom of the page where there was a star next to tiny words that said, "See page 587 for characteristics of the rare and possibly extinct Atlantica Dragon."

Turning to the page, Modo began to read about the Atlantica Dragon. When he finished, he closed the book and looked with wonder at his dragon. Eboo licked remnants of his meal off his nose and began to hum.

Now What?

He can wait forever.
I'm not talking to him!
—GAVIN JOURNAL ENTRY

Modo's life with Eboo had settled into a routine: Get up early to feed Eboo, get ready for school, leave more food for Eboo, go to school, come home and feed Eboo, eat supper, feed Eboo, do homework, play with Eboo, give Eboo a snack, go to bed, start all over again. Modo was exhausted, and Eboo was growing—very fast and very big!

"Dad," Modo said one Saturday morning at breakfast, "what do we do with Eboo now? He can't stay in my room much longer. Have you seen him? He doesn't fit in his cage, his wings need stretching, he needs exercise! And Dad, really, his cage smells like rotten eggs even though I clean it every night! Haven't you smelled it?"

"Now that you mention it, I've noticed a strange odor upstairs," Dad said. "I can take care of that, come on."

Modo followed his father up the narrow wooden stairs to his bedroom.

"Whew!" Dad exclaimed when he opened the door. "No offense, Eboo, but you stink!" Pulling his wand out of his back pocket and holding it above his head, Dad chanted:

"Stinko Winko, smelly too
Fresh air is needed, not smell of poo!"

A soft gray mist floated out of the wand, crossed the room, and went out the window. Modo giggled.

"That's better," Father said, smiling, and reached out to pat Eboo's neck. "Now I smell cinnamon and carnations?"

"That's the same smell that was in Principal Winkleberry's office," Modo observed.

"Interesting," Father said. "He is an amazing creature, Modo. As a kid, I dreamed of dragons, never expecting to see one, much less have one living in my house!" Father headed out the door. "Well, I'm almost done with the bridle for Eboo to wear as he learns to fly. That way we can tether him and keep him out of trouble. Let's go down and finish eating."

"That's cool, can I see it?" Modo asked, following Father down the stairs.

"It's almost ready. I have one or two more straps to attach, and then we can try it on him. I have it in the parking shed. I'll leave it in your room when it's ready."

Gavin came into the kitchen, pushed Finkle off his seat, and slid onto the chair opposite Modo.

"I'm going over to Tad's house to study for the Upper Schola entrance exam. I'll be back later." He drank his orange juice and walked out the kitchen door, letting the screen door slam.

Dad smiled at Modo. "Still not talking to you?" Modo shook his head and lowered it so Dad wouldn't see the wetness in his eyes.

Later that afternoon, Father was sitting on the front porch in one of the blue rockers, reading a book. Father tutored naturals and magicks in reading, and was always looking for new stories to excite his students.

Gavin came out the screen door, letting it slam shut behind him. Always in a hurry, Gavin waved and kept moving.

"Gavin, wait," Father called.

Gavin took two more steps, stopped, and turned around.

"Can I talk to you a minute?" Father asked.

"Okay," Gavin sighed, kicking at fallen pine needles as he came back to the porch.

"I know you're angry about the dragon, but it's not Modo's fault. He didn't ask for this, and frankly, I think he's a bit scared."

"Why should he be scared?" Gavin asked. "He's got a dragon, for Pete's sake!"

"Gavin, this isn't a dragon from your history book or a fairy tale. This is a real dragon—would you know what to do?"

"I guess it could be a bit scary," Gavin admitted.

"Yes," Father said. "And that's why he needs his big brother."

"What for? What can I do?" Gavin asked.

"Be there for him. Give him advice. Let him know you will help him, not abandon him."

Gavin shuffled his feet in the dirt and then plopped down on the porch steps.

"I always thought my gift of growing things was cool. But, Dad, my little brother has a dragon. A dragon! Who cares if I can grow things?"

"Gavin, what gift we have isn't important. It's how or when we use it that matters. Who knows where or why or when your gift will be needed."

"That sounds good, Dad," Gavin said, "but I don't know. I grow big pumpkins and Modo has a dragon—you really think my gift matters?"

"I don't think, Gavin. I know! You never need to feel you're in your brother's shadow, but right now Modo and Eboo need to know you support them. They are both young and have a lot to learn. Will you think about it, please?"

"Yeah, okay," Gavin replied. "I'll think about it."

BULLIES

6

Eboo sure takes a lot of work!
But he's really awesome,
I just wish my friends could meet him.
—MODO JOURNAL ENTRY

Modo put Eboo in his dog crate, which was already becoming too small to hold the growing dragon. Every day it seemed another inch of Eboo's tail stuck out the back of the cage, and his tail spikes were beginning to catch on the wire frame. Standing up was difficult, his body almost touched the sides of the crate, and opening his wings was absolutely impossible!

"I'm going to school now, Eboo," said Modo, setting down a large bucket overflowing with food. "There is plenty of chicken in there, bones and all. I'll be home later and after dark, we can go for a walk." Eboo rustled his wings and blinked at Modo.

"I know you want to fly. Dad is working on a way to keep you safe as you learn. This isn't easy for any of us, okay? See you later."

"*Modo go, Eboo stay, makes for dragging dragon day.*"

Modo grabbed his pack, small journal, and wooden flute and headed out the door for Lower Schola. It was the second week, but already Modo was feeling good about school. The only problem was that he missed his friend Tommy, who wasn't a magick and still went to Anterg Village School, where Modo used to go. Modo hurried down the narrow path, laughing as squirrels criss-crossed in front of him, playing chase up and down the tall pines. Through the trees, he saw Jack, who sat next to him in class. Jack was quiet, smaller than the other boys, and liked to read about nature and the weather.

"Hi, Jack," Modo said. "Did you do your homework?"

"Yeah," Jack replied. "But I would rather read than do math problems, especially when they're about measuring wands and figuring out how many cups of vanishing juice you can get from a one-pound bullfrog."

"You can't get any juice from a bullfrog until he croaks! Ha ha!"

"Hi, Orrin," Modo laughed as Orrin ran to join them, his red hair bouncing with each step. "How can you be so funny this early in the morning?"

"Not sure. It just happens."

The boys continued toward school, talking and laughing. They balanced single file on the stone curbing by the path, waiting to see who would fall off first.

"Hey," Orrin called, "let's cut through the outdoor Show Hall."

The large circular theater had open sides and a large beamed roof that looked like a giant spoked wheel from inside the theater. Wooden backed benches made a semi-circle facing the large stage, where summer performances filled Anterg with laughter and music. Large pine trees stood guard around the theater, casting long shadows across the benches.

Running down the aisles between the benches, the boys raced and jumped for the stage. Sitting on the edge to catch their breaths, they heard voices behind them. Out of the shadows, Gavin and his friends walked up and stood behind the boys.

"Hey, look, some starters on their way to school. I wonder how fast they can run."

"Aw, let's just turn them into frogs," another boy said, "and then we can watch them hop the rest of the way to school." The big boys laughed and pretended to reach for their wands.

The younger boys slid off the stage and stood to wait; Modo wondered if it hurt to be changed into a frog. Jack sniffed, trying not to cry. Orrin whispered, "Could I be something else? I don't like frogs."

"Go ahead, turn them into frogs."

Modo gasped—it was Gavin.

"And then I will turn you into flies for their lunch. Now get going and leave them alone."

The big boys glared at Gavin, jumped off the stage, and pushed past Modo and his friends, giving them each a little shove into the benches.

"C'mon," Gavin said. "Don't just stand there staring at me, let's get to school before we're late. I'll meet you later to walk home."

Eboo Flies

*Now my brother and my friends
are both mad at me!*
—Gavin journal entry

Later that week, Modo and Eboo were in the bedroom. Modo was reading Principal Winkleberry's dragon book to Eboo, who was curled up in a nest of quilts and blankets. On the wall above Modo hung a faded piece of Grandma's music in an old board frame. Modo learned the piece himself and played it when he was alone; it always made him feel better. On the opposite wall, between the windows, hung a poster of old pictures of Anterg. Modo's favorite picture was of kids hanging on a swing out over Hocus Pocus Lake. Behind the door, Modo piled up many, many layers of paper for Eboo's bathroom. Eboo's poop piles were so big, Modo needed a shovel and bucket to clean them up. Every window in Modo's room was open to let the smell escape between Father's de-stinking spells. Unfortunately for Modo, Eboo was a frequent pooper! The bedroom was definitely growing smaller by the day. When Eboo moved around, the wide pine floor boards creaked with every step. Modo was ducking around Eboo's tail when there was a knock at the door.

"Come in," Modo yelled, expecting to see his mom or dad. But it was Gavin who stepped into the room. Modo moved over and stood right in front of Gavin, blocking his way.

"Hey, little brother," Gavin said quietly. "I was wondering, well, could I meet your dragon?"

Modo looked at Gavin for a minute, unsure what to say or feel.

"I guess so," Modo said, glaring at Gavin. "Unless you're going to give me a hard time about him."

"No," Gavin said, "I'm not, honest."

"Okay," Modo said, hesitated a moment, then moved aside. "Eboo, this is Gavin. Gavin, this is Eboo."

"Wow!" Gavin said. "He's really awesome—a dragon, a real live dragon. We studied them in science class, but no one believed they still existed! Can…can I touch him?"

"That's up to Eboo. Reach out your hand palm side up and let him come to you. Oh, and Gavin, in case you haven't heard him, he can talk."

Gavin slowly reached out his hand and waited. Eboo looked at Gavin with his big black eyes and slowly blinked. Then the dragon shuffled forward, laid his snout in Gavin's hand, and began to hum.

Modo smiled and looked up at Gavin, who was grinning.

Eboo backed up, looked at Modo and said, "*Modo has father and Modo has mother. But Eboo and Modo will share this big brother.*"

"Okay then, Gavin," Modo said. "Can you help us figure this out? Dad had to work late and we wanted to try on the bridle. He said Eboo might try flying this week."

Gavin picked up the bridle and looked at the picture in Modo's book. An oval of leather strips slipped over the dragon's snout, with the reins splitting off each side and looped back to the rider.

"Since Eboo is only as tall as me," Gavin said, "we can have him stand up and open his wings so the reins don't get caught on them when we slip it on. Then you can sit on him and we can adjust the length of the reins."

"Okay," Modo said. "Let's give it a try."

"Stand in the middle of the floor, Eboo," Gavin instructed. "Now open your wings."

SMASH! CRASH! BANG! Books slid from shelves, Modo's model castles tumbled to the floor, and socks and shirts flew through the air. The tips of Eboo's wings scraped the bedroom walls, tearing the poster and knocking down pictures, leaving the mirror askew on the wall.

"Yikes!" Gavin yelled. "We can't do this in here! Close your wings, Eboo, close them!"

Eboo closed his wings and sighed. *"Eboo too big. Room too small. There will be no flying at all."*

The boys stood quietly, listening for Mother to come up the stairs. But after a few minutes and no mom, they relaxed.

"Gavin," Modo whispered. "The parking shed—it's empty. He'll fit in there."

"I don't know, Modo. How will we get him down there and then back up here? We better wait for Dad."

"Eboo has flight. Can soar through the night. Down to the ground, without a sound."

"What?" Modo exclaimed. "You already know how to fly? Why didn't you say so? What are we waiting for? We don't need the bridle." Eboo just blinked his big black eyes.

"Slow down, little brother," Gavin said. "Didn't Dad say he had to be kept a secret? What if someone sees him? I think we better wait for Dad. Besides, how are we going to get him outside?"

"The balcony off Mom and Dad's bedroom, it has a big double door. C'mon, Mom's in the kitchen. We can get him to the deck, let him fly a little, and then get him back inside before they know. C'mon, Gavin, let's try it."

"All right, but I still don't think it's a good idea."

Folding Eboo's wings tightly against his body, the boys pushed the dragon through the bedroom door.

"Watch that vase of flowers on the hall table, grab that painting, he's gonna catch it with his tail, duck your head, Eboo, the light!"

Several frantic minutes later, Eboo, Modo, and Gavin stood on the balcony of their parent's bedroom. Mercedes

perched on the railing preening his feathers. He looked at the boys and gave them a warning "*Caw-aw.*"

Modo stroked Eboo's smooth scaly snout. "You promise to come back? You can only fly a short time and no one can see you, okay?"

Eboo rustled his wings, nuzzled Modo's arm, and with a silent rush of air, rose off the deck humming.

DANGER!

8

I hope I don't have to ride Eboo anytime soon.
If I do, everyone will know I'm afraid of heights!
—MODO JOURNAL ENTRY

Eboo disappeared into the moonless sky. Modo and Gavin stood motionless, heads tilted back, eyes searching the night sky for any sign of the dragon. Neither one spoke, their ears alert for unusual sounds. A spray of stars filled the dark purple sky with a soft glow. Below, the plants and animals of Anterg craned just barely upward, watching the flight of a dragon.

Suddenly, headlights began blinking and winking between the trees, climbing the hill toward the house.

"It's Dad!"

The boys walked nonchalantly down the steps past Mom in the kitchen before running out the back door into the yard.

"What are we gonna do? Should we hide? Gavin, what should we do?" Modo paced back and forth across the driveway in front of the parking shed. The shed's double doors were closed, the skinny red boards peeling paint and the rusty hinges weeping dark stains down the sides.

"I told you this wasn't a good idea!" Gavin shouted at Modo.

The roadster turned into the driveway and stopped abruptly when the silhouettes of two boys appeared on the red parking shed door.

"Boys? What are you doing out here? Is Mom okay? Is there a problem?"

"Problem?" Modo whispered, looking at his feet. "Not really a problem."

"Well then, what? Gavin?"

"I met Eboo, Dad, and we were working on his bridle, and well..."

Modo interrupted, "Eboo told us he could already fly, and we brought him out to the balcony, and...and..."

Dad immediately looked up and began turning in every direction, straining to see anything flying in the night sky. The trees stood silent, watching for the dragon too.

"Where is he? Where is Eboo?"

"He should be back any minute. He promised he would come back and not let anyone see him," Modo mumbled.

"Modo, you know the rules—no one, *no one* can know about Eboo. What if he is seen or steals some chickens for dinner or can't find his way back? That's why there was a tether on the bridle!"

Modo stood silently, his shoulders drooping, his eyes
beginning to sting. Slowly, something he had read began
to tease his mind.

Running to the house, Modo yelled, "I'll be right back,
I think I know how to bring him home." After grabbing

his wooden flute in his room, Modo ran back to the yard, the screen door slamming like a shot in the night.

"If Eboo is the kind of dragon I think he is, the music will bring him back," Modo said.

Gavin rolled his eyes. Dad stood to the side with his arms crossed, frowning.

Modo pushed his glasses up and began to play the flute. The soft sound floated through the night, filling the spaces between the trees and rocks like an evening fog. Gently, the melody began to rise and then fall back to once again begin the climb. The haunting tune climbed above the treetops, soared to the stars, and swirled across the universe. Modo's fingers felt weightless as they moved over the holes, his breath strong but gentle. With his eyes closed, Modo could see the music hanging on his bedroom wall and was once again comforted by the melody. Building the song to its musical climax, Modo then played the tune to a quiet end.

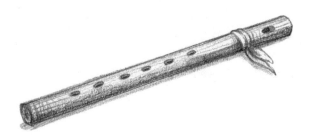

Gavin's mouth hung open, speechless for once.

Father's arms hung limply at his side. "Modo, where did you learn that?" he asked, staring at his younger son.

"It's Grandma's music that hangs on the wall in my room. It was in the bag with my flute. Mom framed it for me; it's named 'A Dragon's Wish.' But it doesn't usually sound this good."

Whoosh, whoosh, whoosh.

A gentle breeze ruffled Modo's dark curly hair as Eboo landed quietly in the driveway.

"Eboo hears a Call, from Modo's flute so small. He will always come a-winging when Modo's flute is singing."

Dad ran across the driveway to Modo and Eboo.

"We'll talk about the music later," Dad said in a quiet voice. "Eboo will stay in the parking shed tonight, and Modo, you can stay with him. Neither of you is to leave— do you understand?"

"Yes," Modo whispered.

"Gavin, tomorrow we will go and find a place for Eboo, close by, but hidden. Now, everyone to bed!"

Eboo rustled his wings and nudged Father's arm. Father turned and looked at the dragon. Eboo's black eyes stared at Father for several seconds.

"Eboo did fly, but all is not well. Near the Watchtower, Gorlings I smell."

Warning

Gorlings! We read about them in history class.
This is bad.
—Gavin journal entry

Father stared at Eboo a moment, then opened the parking shed doors.

"Dad," Modo asked. "What are the Gorlings? Where do they come from? How did Eboo smell them?"

"Inside, Modo," Father said, looking around the yard. "You too, Eboo."

"Dad, tell me, what are they?"

"Not tonight, Modo. Right now you and Eboo need to get inside. No more discussion, I mean it!"

Father and Gavin headed into the house after closing the parking shed door with Modo and Eboo safely inside. The shed walls were dusty, and splinters of light from the back porch lantern slipped through gaps in the boards.

Corners of the shed were thick with gauzy webs, some with large spiders suspended in their centers. Rakes, hoes, and shovels hung on the walls next to two-wheeled pedalers. In the middle of the floor was a stain from roadster leaks. One corner held a tower of flower pots leaning crookedly to the right.

Eboo turned himself in circles several times before settling down on some old green tattered moving pads. When he was comfortable, Modo curled up next to him and whispered, "What is a Gorling?"

"Time for Modo and Eboo to sleep; no talk of Gorlings, not one more peep. Plenty of time when comes the sun to decide if we should stay or run."

Inside the house, Father, Mother, and Gavin sat around the old wooden kitchen table where Finkle was napping. The night song of crickets and cicadas clicked and chirped through the screen door, accenting Gavin and Father's silence.

Finally, Gavin began explaining everything to Mother, whose eyes grew wider and wider as Gavin continued talking. Then Father repeated Eboo's words:

"Eboo did fly, but all is not well. Near the Watchtower, Gorlings I smell."

Mother gasped and jumped out of her seat, knocking over her chair, scaring Finkle onto the floor.

"Gorlings? Can it be true?"

"We need to stay calm," Father said. "Perhaps this is why Eboo is here, but I don't want to scare Modo until we know more. Tomorrow Gavin and I will find a secret place for Eboo to live. He was at the Watchtower, so the Gorlings, if they are back, could be anywhere within fifteen miles, not necessarily right here. Not yet. Now, how about some of your good lemonade? That always makes us feel better."

Gavin spoke up. "I've been thinking, Dad. I thought the deserted carousel building might be a good spot for Eboo, but it is a bit close to the shops in the village. Then I remembered Old Turtle Pond. There is a cave close by that is well hidden. I wouldn't even know about it, except that I was following a fox one day and it appeared to suddenly vanish."

"Good thinking, Gavin. We'll check it out in the morning."

Mother walked over to the cold cupboard and took out a pitcher of lemonade, the preferred drink of magicks. She filled three glasses, carried two back to the table, and went back for the third. Picking up a glass, Gavin walked over to the screen door and stood quietly looking out at the trees and stars.

"Dad," Gavin asked, "what do Gorlings smell like?"

"I read a long time ago that they emit a strong odor of cucumbers."

"Cucumbers?"

"Yes, cucumbers. If I remember correctly, as the evil thoughts take stronger root in their being, it changes their skin to smell like cucumbers. Dragons are apparently very sensitive to the smell, as are some magicks. But for now, no mention of the Gorlings to anyone!"

A HOME FOR EBOO

I don't want Eboo to move.
I'd rather have a poopy, stinky room than him gone.
—MODO JOURNAL ENTRY

"C'mon, Eboo. We're going to walk you to your new home," Modo said quietly as he opened the parking shed doors.

It was a cloudy night several days after Eboo's first flight. Days and nights in the shed had made the dragon restless, eager to fly again.

"Okay, boys. We'll stay on the back streets until we're clear of the village, and keep to the woods when possible. Gavin, remember as you choose the way that Eboo is almost as tall as you, but quite a bit wider. Eboo will follow you and Modo, I'll be behind Eboo." Father whistled quietly and Mercedes landed silently on his shoulder.

"Fly ahead, Mercedes. Let us know if there is anyone who might see us." Clicking his beak in answer, the crow took off, heading for Old Turtle Pond.

It was after midnight, and the houses were dark except for an occasional porch lantern. All was quiet. The smell of pine was strong; the cottages seemed to be holding their breath, waiting with closed curtain eyes for the group to pass. Eboo's tail swept the dry leaves aside, leaving a distinct path, but Father gently waved his wand from side to side, watching as the leaves returned to their original places. Father's lips barely moved as he chanted:

Back in place, there to stay. Leave no trace we came this way.

Ten minutes later, Gavin turned off the road and followed a wide dirt path into the woods. Tree branches

reached across the path, forming a tunnel into the pond. Modo moved back beside Eboo and laid his hand on the dragon's long neck. The sound of water gurgling out of the pond and into a creek joined the rustle of poplar leaves, whispering the secret of the dragon in their woods. Mercedes perched quietly in a nearby oak, watching the procession. As they walked past Old Turtle Pond, a breeze blew off the water, making Modo shiver.

Gavin moved slowly past the old well at the far end of the pond. The well was constructed of granite stones, edges rounded by time and covered in moss. The edge of the well was level with the ground, keeping it hidden and making it easy to miss.

Gavin disappeared behind a large bush into a thicket. "Come through. I'll light the way with my wand," he said.

Modo, Eboo, and Father followed Gavin into a huge open room. The cave roof was high enough for Eboo and Father to stand comfortably inside. The walls, carved from sandstone by centuries of water, were cool to the touch. Although the dirt floor was dry, with a slight incline toward the mouth of the cave, the rock room smelled like the damp decaying ground of the forest floor. The thicket muted any sounds from outside the cave, making the silence feel like another presence inside.

"I brought some hay bales in yesterday so Eboo has a place to sleep."

"Thank you, Gavin," Modo said quietly.

Father walked to the back of the cave hunting for any hidden passages or entrances. Satisfied that there were none, he came back to the boys.

"Eboo, you can only hunt at night. No farm animals—there can be no evidence that you are here. No one can even suspect that you exist. Fly over the Blue Mountains and hunt in the game lands on the other side. Modo will come every night to see you and bring extra food. Stay away from Nonabel."

"Eboo will stay and sleep all day. At night, Eboo flies in deep purple skies."

Modo would miss waking up to the dragon sleeping under the framed music, so he pulled his wooden flute from his back pocket and began to play "A Dragon's Wish." For the first time, Eboo began to hum along, matching Modo's flute note for note. The eerie melody filled the cave and wrapped around them, rising and falling. The air began to shimmer, wrapping itself around Modo and Eboo, forming an unbreakable bond between them. They were now companions for life.

"Modo," Father whispered, "your music is your connection to Eboo. You must carry your flute with you…always."

TEAS AND TALES

Some people are just weird!
—MODO JOURNAL ENTRY

Father, Gavin, and Modo were on their way to the Teas and Tales Bookstore in Nonabel. Father was picking up books for his students, and Modo and Gavin knew Father would always buy them books too. As they approached Nonabel, the farm fields began to sprout more and more houses, and soon the old deserted foundry came into view. The brick foundry closed a few years before Gavin was born. Modo thought the old decrepit building looked like a dark, dirty dungeon. It gave him the creeps.

Soon they arrived on the main road through Nonabel. Father turned into a tree-lined roadster lot and parked under a chestnut tree. Walking down the streets in Nonabel always made Modo nervous. The buildings were tall and made of brick and stone. The structures seemed to be leaning over, frowning at those walking below. There were so many roadsters and pedalers zipping through the streets, so many people walking in every direction, Modo felt caught in a maze.

"Here we are," Father said, stepping under the wide, black-and-white striped awning and opening the yellow screen door to Teas and Tales.

Modo loved the bookstore; it felt like a small piece of Anterg in the middle of the city. Small blue-and-white wooden tables with matching chairs were scattered around the front of the store. Sugar bowls and small vases of fresh flowers sat on lacy doilies in the center of each table. A glass cabinet at the end of the sales counter was filled with all kinds of cookies and scones. Modo and Gavin loved the molasses cookies best. Behind the counter were shelves full of jars of tea and delightfully mismatched tea cups, plates, and saucers. On one end of a wide counter below the teas sat a metal hot water dispenser. On the other end there was a tall glass jar of lemonade for the magicks and one of sweet tea for the naturals. The rest of the store was filled with shelves and shelves of books, art supplies, and cozy places to sit and read. Modo thought it would be a wonderful place to work someday.

"Okay," Father said. "Go find your books and I'll meet you at one of the tables with lemonade and cookies."

Modo knew exactly what book he wanted, *A Pictorial Compendium of Dragons.* Even before Eboo arrived, Modo had often looked through the book. Now, more than ever, he wanted to own it—and he wanted to share it with Eboo. Picking the volume gently off the shelf, Modo headed to a table in the front. Father wasn't there yet, so he chose a table. He noticed a woman sitting at the next table, her blonde hair bouncing in wild curls off her head. She was wearing a bright yellow dress and glared at him briefly when he looked at her. Modo hung his jacket on a chair and sat down with his back to her.

Modo was slowly paging through his book when Gavin plopped down next to him.

"What did you pick?" Modo asked.

"It's a book about gardening," Gavin said. "I want to try growing some new things next year."

"Oh," Modo said with a laugh, "like pumpkins that don't break when you move them?"

"Very funny," Gavin replied. "What did you get?"

"I've wanted this dragon book for a long time!" Modo blurted out excitedly. "I didn't realize there were so many kinds of dragons besides Atlantica dragons!"

Father sat down, placing a tray of cookies and lemonades on the table. He frowned.

"Modo. That's enough. Say no more."

Just then, the woman at the next table dropped her napkin under Modo's chair. Leaning over to pick it up, she began to sniffle and then sneezed.

"Excuse me," she said tersely. "Something tickled my nose."

Father also reached to pick up the napkin, sniffed, and suddenly stiffened. Seeing the tall glass of lemonade on her table, he said, "Let's finish up our treats and get going."

Gavin showed Father his gardening book, looked at Father, and tapped his nose. Father barely nodded and then stood to leave.

"Wait," Modo said. "Can I show you a book, Dad? We don't need to get it today, but it would be perfect for Tommy's birthday. You know how he's always collecting rocks and making sculptures with them? Well, there's a book about stone sculptures and stone artists in history."

"Okay," Father said. "Let's get it now and pay for the books and treats and head home."

The ride home to Anterg was quiet as both boys looked through their books. Gavin, sitting in the front, glanced over at Father a few times, but returned to his book when Father didn't look back.

"Shoot," Modo said suddenly.

"What's the matter?" Father asked.

"I left my jacket on the chair in the store."

"I'm sure they'll save it for us," Father said. "I'll get it next time I'm in town."

"Hey, did anyone else smell something weird in there?" Modo asked.

Father looked at Gavin and shook his head.

GORLINGS

12

Warneke's large brick house stood on the outskirts of Nonabel near old deserted foundry buildings. Tall and narrow, the house dared anyone to walk by without speeding up or looking nervously at the shadow moving across a window. Despite the gloomy look of the house, the gardens were wild with color. Roses exploded on large bushes, sunflowers stood like yellow sentries, and lilies grew rampant in every available space.

Warneke paced the floor of her large living room, her footsteps leaving an indented path on the blue flowered carpet. Dressed in a long orange dress that made her seem even taller than she was, Warneke's crazy blonde hair corkscrewed in all directions off her head, which ached like wearing a hat that was too tight. Worst of all was the sneezing! Something in the air had changed, and now she was constantly sneezing. It all began in the bookstore when she picked up her napkin under that boy's chair, the boy with the dragon book. She was sure she heard him mention Atlantica dragons, but that seemed crazy. But when she got close to his jacket, something happened. Picking up the gray jacket and sniffing it, Warneke began sneezing repeatedly.

"Noooooo!" Warneke screamed. "No, it can't be! *Constantly sneezing?* Constantly sneezing! Carnations and cinnamon—the jacket smells of carnations and cinnamon!"

As the oldest living magick, Warneke sometimes forgot things from long ago. But now she remembered. The only thing that made her constantly sneeze was carnations and cinnamon, the smell of dragons—specifically Atlantica dragons!

One thing Warneke never forgot was the last time she led the Gorlings in an attempt to take over Anterg. Warneke and her brother Dunmore were magicks, as was their father, but their mother was a natural. Although her brother adored their mother, Warneke despised her as a weak, ungifted natural woman. Her hatred of her mother convinced Warneke that naturals and magicks shouldn't live together in the same communities. Warneke began capturing naturals and, using her violin playing, torturing and enslaving them. Magicks who agreed with Warneke became her workers, known as Gorlings. The Gorlings used the enslaved naturals as servants and workers in their mines and foundries. But the magicks and naturals in Anterg fought back, convinced that they were stronger and better together.

Finally fed up with the constant small skirmishes in Anterg, Warneke and the Gorlings planned a final, unescapable assault. One night, the Gorlings coordinated their attacks and set fires in multiple places around Anterg. There were so many fires and so many Gorlings that even the magicks couldn't keep up with them, despite extinguishing many of the fires.

The Gorlings planned the fires so the villagers had nowhere to go but Hocus Pocus Lake. Warneke began playing her violin as the first naturals arrived at the lake. The naturals fell to the ground in agony. She was delighted to see the lake filled with folks—families holding their children above the water, and the elders floating in canoes at the center of the lake.

Then Warneke noticed that the entire outer rim of villagers were musicians—naturals and magicks—holding their instruments. On the bank, Warneke played her violin in earnest, but she was soon overwhelmed when all the musicians began playing the Anthem of Anterg, all together. It soon became apparent that one magick, a large man playing a silver trumpet, was leading the group. The notes of the anthem soared from Winkleberry's instrument, across the lake and over the Blue Mountains. The music was a passionate cry for help.

Warneke was dismayed as the intensity of the villagers' music began to weaken her power, and soon the trumpet Call was answered. Warneke faltered as, from across the lake, a large white dragon flew toward them, with more dragons in its wake. The dragons landed on the shore, dozens of them, their great wings casting jagged shadows from the flames, encircled the lake, and began to hum the Anthem. Warneke faltered. Try as she might, she could not outplay the villagers and the dragons. The heat and flames of the fire closed in on her and the Gorlings, but when they moved toward the water for relief, the dragons stepped forward and stopped them.

Warneke remembered the feeling of dismay and failure when she and the Gorlings magicked themselves out of the flames. Her followers scattered, defeated and scared of revenge that might come to them. Warneke traveled for many decades, meeting with magicks in other countries and learning, rebuilding her power, finally returning to Nonabel ten years ago, where she quietly worked to restore the Gorling membership. She wasn't about to let Anterg and a new generation of magicks and naturals stop her again!

"*Achoo!* Julian, come here. I have a job for you."

A short, bald man with an uneven step hurried into the room, tripped on the carpet, and landed facedown at Warneke's feet.

"Yes, mistress," he mumbled into the rug.

"Get up, you bumbling idiot. *Achoo!* How I chose you for my servant is beyond me!"

"Yes, mistress." Julian clambered to his feet and bowed.

"I need you to find a boy named Tommy; he lives in Anterg and collects rocks. *A-a-a-choo!* Find him and follow him. See if he ever meets with a magick boy, one with dark curly hair who wears blue wire glasses. Report back to me where he goes and who he hangs out with. I can't be seen in Anterg. The magick boy's father saw me and already seemed suspicious—I can't risk it. And put that jacket in the attic!"

"Yes, mistress, right away." Julian grabbed the jacket, turned to leave, caught his sleeve on a corner table, and dumped the lamp on the floor. He scrambled to pick it up and hurried out the door.

Warneke crossed the room, opened a black case, and took out a violin.

"We'll see what this Tommy can tell us. He may know nothing, but even so we will use him to lure the magick boy. And once we have him, we can find that dragon. Boys and dragons are hard to keep apart!"

As Julian stepped outside the room, the screeches and screams of Warneke's playing filled the house with anger and frustration.

TOMMY

13

I wish I could talk to Tommy about Eboo.
He would love him, I know it!
—MODO JOURNAL ENTRY

Modo decided to leave a little early to visit Eboo so he could stop for a treat at the Scoop-dee-doo or grab a drink at the Village Store. The sun was just setting as Modo set out on a deer path through the woods along a small creek. The water skipped around rocks, slowed behind fallen logs, and scooted under bridges of tree roots. Modo followed the stream until he came to a place where the rocks made a stepping-stone path across the water. Hopping from one foot to the other across the stones, Modo landed on the other side and turned onto a narrow street leading into the village.

Thinking about how to find out more about the Gorlings, Modo wasn't paying attention to his surroundings. As he walked past the Scoop-dee-doo Ice Cream Shop and turned toward the Village Store, he heard his name.

Glancing behind him, Modo saw some of the boys from Gavin's class.

"Hey, flute boy," they called. "Play us a song."

Modo ignored the boys and kept walking.

"C'mon, flutey, play something for us!" The boys sounded closer.

"Modo, hey, Modo! Over here!"

It was Tommy, Modo's friend from the Anterg Village School, walking down the other side of the street. Modo ran across to Tommy and watched as the older boys laughed and pointed at him as they went into the Village Store.

"Thanks, Tommy. Those boys know they can't use magick except in defense, so I doubt they would have hurt me. But you never know. Thanks for distracting them. How are you doing? Still collecting rocks?"

"Yeah," said Tommy, setting down three flat rocks. "School isn't as much fun without you, though. How do you like magick school? Is it hard?"

"Well," Modo replied, "some things are the same, and then there are magick things like wands and potions. But they don't let us do much except in magick lab. First years can't even take wands home until after the winter break."

"Can you make things disappear?" Tommy asked. "That would be cool!"

"Not very well," Modo said. "Sometimes we can get things to disappear, but we can't get them back." Modo laughed. "I guess that's why we can't take our wands home yet!"

"Yeah," Tommy said, grinning, "Jack would probably disappear his little sister permanently."

"But we're getting good at moving things."

"Can you move a roadster?" Tommy asked, wide-eyed.

"No," Modo answered. "But the other day I lifted a tea cup and put it back down without breaking it. That was a first!" Tommy laughed.

"I bet your rock collection's getting really big," Modo said, looking at the rocks at Tommy's feet.

"It is," Tommy answered. "I really like making my animals. It's fun and Mom likes them in her garden."

"I'll tell my mom about them," Modo said. "I bet she'd like one for her garden too. Well, thanks, again, I have to get going."

"Wait, where are you going?" Tommy asked. "Can we get together sometime? Can we still be friends?"

Tommy looked at Modo, worry wrinkling around his brown eyes.

"Of course." Modo smiled. "I just have a magick errand I need to run right now. I'll be in touch soon, I have a birthday present for you. And Tommy—" Modo hesitated. "Tommy, be careful." Modo ran off down a dark alley.

"Be careful?" Tommy stood and watched Modo disappear into the darkness between two old cottages.

As Tommy walked slowly back into the village, he heard someone knock over a trash can across the street.

PRINCIPAL WINKLEBERRY

I wonder if principals were ever kids!
—MODO JOURNAL ENTRY

"Modo Malarkey, please report to the principal's office. Modo Malarkey to the principal's office."

"Uh oh," Jack said. "What did you do?"

"Nothing," Modo said. "At least nothing I remember!"

"Right," Orrin said. "Are you holding out on us?"

"No, really!" Modo exclaimed. "I haven't done anything."

He hurried down the hall, his stomach flip-flopping with each step.

"Here you are," Principal Winkleberry said when Modo walked into the outer office. "Come in, come in."

After shutting his heavy office door, Principal Winkleberry sat down behind his big desk and smiled.

The corners of a new plaid bow tie winked out on the sides of his chin. A wool vest was buttoned over his roundness, straining to hold it inside, the silver dragon pendant caught on a button. Once again, Modo smelled the faint scent of cinnamon and carnations in the room. In the corner, a silver trumpet lay in an open case.

"Sit down, Modo. Relax, you haven't done anything wrong. I'm wondering how you are getting along with your dragon."

"Oh," said Modo, relaxing into a soft, flowered armchair. "We're doing fine, sir. He sure eats a lot. He's getting big—and he flies."

"Anything else about Eboo that surprises you?"

"Well, sir, I've never had a dragon before, so everything surprises me. I didn't know he could fly until he told me. He only talks in rhymes, you know," Modo said.

"Only in rhymes, you say?" Principal Winkleberry stroked his chin. "Interesting. And has he started humming yet?"

"Why yes, he has," Modo replied. "It's pretty cool how he can hum everything I play on my flute."

"He hums what you play? He talks in rhymes? He flies already? Well, thank you, Modo. You can return to class now—off you go." Principal Winkleberry stood up, hurried around the desk, and practically pushed Modo out the door.

Modo arrived back to class just in time for morning break, wondering what that meeting was all about.

Principal Winkleberry stood at his office window watching Modo and his friends in the play area, once again fingering the silver dragon. He smiled as he thought of the possibilities. He was thrilled when the little dragon appeared during Modo's test for Lower Schola, but also a bit wistful. If what the boy said was true, not only had the first dragon in almost a century returned, he was an Atlantica dragon! He would work with the boy, but not until some questions were answered: What danger brought the dragon? And why did he choose Modo?

RESEARCH

*If Dad, Mom, and Gavin won't tell me,
I'll find out myself!*
—MODO JOURNAL ENTRY

The next Saturday, Modo decided to spend the afternoon reading in the cave with Eboo. Entering through the thicket covering the mouth of the cave, Modo shivered as the cool dampness crawled up his arms. To one side, on a scattered pile of hay, Eboo was curled up, snout lying across his front feet, his tail wrapped around his green side. The spikes on Eboo's back rose and fell slowly as he breathed in and out, a low, soft snore humming through the cave. Modo sat down on one of the sleeping bags, opened his pack, and pulled out *A History of Magick Wars and Enemies*. Pushing up his glasses, Modo turned to the index and finally found what he was looking for: The Gorlings, 94.

Silently he read:

The Gorlings are a self-named group of magicks determined to enslave naturals and to neutralize the powers of other magicks who protect naturals. Gorlings believe magicks and naturals should not live together as families or even in the same communities. They fear a weakening of their powers if they live with naturals. Many Gorlings channel their magickal influence through music and art, enslaving naturals before they realize what has happened. The only possible way to defeat a Gorling is through the art form they magickally use.

The Gorlings went into hiding many years ago after the defeat of their leader, Warneke, at the Fire of Hocus Pocus Lake (see page 245). In the village of Anterg, the naturals and magicks worked together to defeat Warneke by outplaying her violin and aided by the humming of Atlantica dragons led by Dreyken. Although the magick connected to Dreyken is known to some, this person's identity is kept secret as protection from any remaining Gorlings.

Many believe the Gorlings are hiding in plain view among the population. Interestingly, as they become more powerful, they emit an odor that can be detected by some magicks and dragons.

A grainy black-and-white photo showed a tall woman with crazy hair playing the violin. Although he couldn't see her face in the picture, there was something familiar about the woman, something unsettling.

Modo shut the book, leaned back against Eboo, and closed his eyes as one thought after another bounced through his brain. So this Warneke was behind the Gorlings, and she used a violin to hurt people. There was a fire at Hocus Pocus Lake, and there were other humming dragons. Did Eboo know Dreyken? And whatever were he and Eboo supposed to do? He was only a boy with a flute!

Slowly the warmth of Eboo's body calmed Modo's mind, and the slow rhythm of the dragon's breathing lulled him to sleep. Together the boy and dragon slept away the afternoon.

When Modo woke, he was surprised to see Gavin sitting nearby, leaning against the cave wall.

"Hey, Gavin." Modo yawned. "What are you doing here?"

"We couldn't find you, so Dad sent Mercedes to look for you. We thought you might be here."

"I read about the Gorlings—why wouldn't Father tell me?"

"He didn't want to scare you. He doesn't want you to do something stupid—you know, with Eboo."

"We have to do something. And Eboo is an Atlantica dragon."

"You're right, but you are both young and you both need training before you can do anything. We just have to hope they don't get organized before the magicks and naturals can prepare.

"How do we know who is a Gorling and who isn't?" Modo asked.

"I think we're going to have to depend on Eboo for that. But then again, we can't let Eboo be seen."

"This is impossible." Modo sighed. "What good is having a dragon if he can't help us?"

He pulled out his flute and began to play. After several folk tunes, Modo began to play "A Dragon's Wish." Eboo began to stir. When Modo stopped, Eboo said, *"Modo plays my Call many, many times. Eboo wants to know the words, wants to know the rhymes."*

Modo quietly began to sing:
I fly above the Watchtower
beyond the blue-green earth.
The music of the universe sings to me since birth:
Bring my children together,
may all conflict cease.
Let all creatures live in freedom,
let all creatures live in peace.

TAKEN

16

*Sometimes I wish I was a magick
or Modo was a natural.*
—TOMMY JOURNAL ENTRY

Warneke's violin was wailing before Julian ever got in the
door. Sticking his fingers in his ears and wincing, Julian
waited for the high-pitched squeals to stop.

"Well," Warneke screamed. "Did you learn anything
at all?"

"I found the natural boy. He walks to school and
home, and often walks the village at dusk. But he has not
met the magick boy again. He spends time collecting rocks
and piling them up."

"I'm tired of waiting," Warneke growled through
gritted teeth. "Get the boy and bring him here. And don't
get caught!"

"Yes, mistress."

Julian headed for the door, muttering under his breath. Suddenly the violin screeched unbearably, and he fell to the floor, wincing in pain.

"Do you want to say something?" Warneke shouted.

Julian shook his head as he tried to get up on his knees and crawl out of the room.

"I expect you and the boy back here within the hour!"

Tommy went out around dusk, gathering rocks for his collection and hoping to find Modo. Several times in the last weeks he had spotted Modo moving through the village. He spied him through the trees at the Village Store and, on his birthday, he met Modo and Gavin for a treat on the wide porch of the Scoop-dee-doo Ice Cream Shop. Modo gave him an awesome book about rock sculptors as a birthday present. But since that night, Modo didn't do more than wave to him in passing. Tommy missed his friend—at least he thought he was still his friend. Anyway, he needed to talk to him. He thought someone was watching him, and he was scared.

Tommy sat down on one of the benches scattered throughout the village. Last year Tommy and Modo did everything together. Some of the best times were hiking through the woods around Anterg. They packed lunches, Tommy brought his rock bag, and Modo brought his flute. One time, they hiked up to the Watchtower. Tommy laughed remembering how he wanted to eat lunch on top of the tower and how Modo finally confessed he was afraid of heights. So they sat at the base of the tower, ate lunch, and talked. Sometimes Modo would play his flute while Tommy searched for interesting rocks. Everything always worked out because they had each other to depend on. Now Tommy didn't know what to think. Modo was nice enough, but he just didn't seem to have any time for Tommy.

Tommy walked around the village several times looking for Modo. Eventually he headed for the Old Carousel Building. The large round structure stood in an old grove of trees behind the village shops. The once sliding sides, now gray with a few patches of peeling white paint, were frozen in rust on metal rails. Tall ferns and yellow-flowered bushes grew up all around and under the building.

Tommy slipped in through a loose board on the back side. The air was damp and thick with the dust of laughter and memories. The old ticket booth stood to one side, its cracked, faded red-and-blue sign hanging sideways from one nail. On the far side, a long metal arm stretched out of the darkness toward the platform. Extended from the end was a metal ring, a prize riders could reach out and try to grab as they circled around.

Tommy and Modo played many times in the old building when they went to school together. All the colorful, wooden carved animals were gone to museums and collectors, but the large circular blue platform was still there, and some of the poles were still bolted to the platform. Tommy and Modo would weave in and out of them, racing to see who could get around the circle first.

A small shaft of sun, filled with floating motes, descended from a hole in the circular roof onto the platform. Tommy sat down in the puddle of light, wondering what to do.

Creak, creak, creak—crash! "Owww!"

"Who's there? Modo?" Tommy stood up and ran for the loose board to get out.

He screamed as something was thrown over his head, enveloping him in darkness. His arms pinned to his sides, he was raised off his feet and swiftly carried away. Suddenly the air turned cooler as the person carrying him stumbled and then dropped him onto a hard surface. A lid slammed shut above him, an engine started, and then he was moving. He kicked and yelled as the roadster roared down the road.

WARNEKE

17

What would happen
if I told Modo,
or his dad, or Gavin?
I'm just too scared of Warneke!
—TOMMY JOURNAL ENTRY

Tommy was dumped onto a carpeted floor and a jacket removed from his head. Afraid to open his eyes, Tommy didn't move, waiting for what would happen next.

"Open your eyes, boy," a sharp voice ordered.

Tommy heard footsteps behind him and turned to see a tall woman dressed in bright purple from the scarf around her crazy blonde head to her knee-high boots.

Tommy sat up and looked around the room. There was little light, as all the window shades were closed and only small lamps were lit on the tables, casting strange shadows on the windows and walls. The room was filled with old pieces of furniture, a large sofa with wooden legs, and tables covered with small statues of woodland animals, many of them foxes. On the walls, paintings of flowers brought small spots of bright color to the gloomy room. A tall clock standing in the corner began chiming a soft repeating *bonnnng, bonnnng, bonnnng.*

"Get up, natural," the woman said, sneering. Tommy scrambled to his feet, though his legs were shaking and his heart pounded so loudly in his ears he was sure the woman could hear it.

"Tell me about the magick boy," she commanded.

"What magick boy?" Tommy answered.

"The one Julian saw you with the other evening in Anterg," the woman said, glaring at Tommy.

"I have lots of friends, naturals and magicks. I'm not sure which one you're talking about," Tommy said.

The woman walked across the room and picked up a violin. Placing it under her chin, she played one long, sustained screeching note.

Tommy thought his head was going to explode. The pain seared through his brain and he fell to the floor.

"Shall we try again?" the woman asked. "What is the magick boy's name?"

"Why do you want to know?" Tommy asked.

"Okay," said the woman, lifting the violin to her chin.

"No," Tommy said, "wait."

"That's better," the woman said.

"You might mean Modo," Tommy whispered, a tear slowly rolling down his cheek as he sat up.

"Ah, well, now I have a name. Where does he live?"

"In Anterg, near the Racket Park. Why do you want to know about Modo?" Tommy asked.

"None of your business, natural," she replied.

"Wha-what do you want with me? I didn't get into Lower Schola, I'm not a magick. I don't have any gifts."

"One thing I have learned, natural—although magick gifts are very strong, naturals possess powerful gifts, also. The trick is knowing what kind of gift you possess."

Tommy was confused. Why would this magick want him, and how was Modo involved?

"Now, Tommy, I'm going to ask you a question, and only the truth will be accepted. Do you understand?"

Tommy nodded.

"Good. Does Modo have a dragon?"

"A dragon? *No!*"

Instantly Warneke lifted her violin and, placing it under her chin, began to play. A blinding pain raced through his body, making it impossible to breathe. Tommy screamed and fell to the floor again, pulling his knees to his chest, tears flowing down his cheeks and onto the blue carpet. Rolling onto his side, blackness closing in, Tommy was sure he was going to pass out. And just as suddenly, it stopped. Tommy gasped for air.

Warneke placed the violin back in the case.

"Now, I'll ask once again. Does Modo have a dragon?"

"I don't know," Tommy said, sobbing. "I've only seen him twice since school started. He didn't say anything about a dragon. Please, I don't know."

"Julian," Warneke called. A small man stumbled in immediately. "Take him back, before he is missed. But you, boy, are going back with a job to do: follow Modo and find out if he does have a dragon and where he is keeping it. And not a word about seeing me! Do you understand?"

"Yes," Tommy whispered.

"If you try to trick me, not only will you never go home, you will watch and see how much your mother likes my violin music. Then you will both be sent to the foundry where you will be my slaves for the rest of your lives—hot sparks falling on your skin, tongues coated with ash, eyes blinded by the intense fires. Is that clear?"

Tommy nodded, unable to speak.

"Julian, return him to Anterg. Stay close by and see that he fulfills his mission."

"Yes, mistress. C'mon, boy."

Julian turned and walked right into the door frame, smashing his nose. Tommy grabbed his hand and pulled him through before Warneke could get the violin to her chin.

A Bad Man

18

Can I trust Julian?
I don't want to be bad like him.
—TOMMY JOURNAL ENTRY

Julian climbed into the roadster, rubbing his nose. Tommy stood quietly sniffing as tears dripped off his face. He turned and took a few steps away from the roadster.

"Don't even think about escaping," Julian warned. "She shows no mercy."

Tommy turned back and climbed in the front seat next to Julian.

As the roadster traveled through Nonabel and out into the farmlands, Tommy stared out the window.

"You're a bad man," Tommy whispered.

Julian was quiet for several minutes. "Yes, I am—now. But I was good once, long ago."

"Why do you help her?" Tommy asked.

"You felt what she can do with her violin."

"Yes, but you kidnapped me, you help her scare and hurt people!"

"What would you suggest? Running away? Escaping? It's not that easy."

Julian was again quiet as they rode along the wooded road to Anterg. Parking near Racket Park, Julian looked over at Tommy.

"One time I didn't come back," he said. "I ran away to the Miehnam Mountains, sure I could never be found there. I didn't even tell my wife where I was. But Warneke has spies everywhere, even among the animals—especially Ren, her gray-tailed red fox. The Gorlings eventually found me. When they delivered me to Warneke, she had my wife. I was forced to watch as they tortured her with fire balls and stinging sprays from their wands. When the Gorlings were done with her, Warneke started in with the violin. The violin was so bad, it damaged my ears so my balance is off. That's why I'm so clumsy. That just makes her angrier. When she stopped, they dragged me away and locked me in a room. The last thing I heard was my wife screaming. I don't know where she is, or if she's even alive."

"I'm sorry," Tommy whispered. Julian and Tommy sat quietly for several minutes.

"I'll be around," Julian said. "Remember what you're to do?"

"Yes," Tommy said. "Spy on my best friend."

Julian reached over and squeezed Tommy's shoulder. "Now I'm sorry," he said.

Tommy climbed out of the roadster and headed home.

MAGICAL GIFTS

Could my gift be something other than my music,
and other than Eboo? This is scary!
—MODO JOURNAL ENTRY

"Attention: First-year students are required
to attend a Saturday morning meeting tomorrow
regarding their unique magical gifts.
This is mandatory! 9 a.m. sharp!"

Jack, Orrin, and Modo looked at each other and shrugged.

"Do either of you know what your gift is?" Jack asked. "'Cause I sure don't know mine. I always hoped that if I was a magick my gift would be to control my little sister."

Modo and Orrin grinned. "I don't think it works that way," Orrin said with a laugh. "I didn't really know about the gifts until I got to Lower Schola. I just thought my dad was a superhero because he was so strong and could lift just about anything."

"Well," Jack said, "I have no idea what my gift might be."

"I have an idea what mine might be," Modo muttered.

Orrin and Jack both nodded.

"Yeah, we think we know what yours is too—music. You don't go anywhere without your flute."

"Oh, ah, yeah, my flute," Modo answered. "Well, I guess we'll find out tomorrow!"

The next morning all the new students stood around the Activity Hall in small groups, wondering what their gift would be and how they would find out. The room began to warm up as sun streamed in through windows high on the wall. The large open floor was marked with lines for various games. Groups of girls in dresses and skirts were standing in small clusters on one side of the room. Boys and girls in jeans and shorts mingled in clumps throughout the space. Here and there a single student stood, or a pair quietly talked.

When Modo and Jack arrived, they searched around the large room for Orrin.

"I hope my gift is healing," Modo heard someone say in a group of girls huddled together. "Well, I hope mine has to do with animals," said another girl.

"Over there," Jack said, pointing to the far side of the room. "There's Orrin." Orrin was standing alone near the far wall where chairs were stacked in small towers.

"Hey, Orrin," Modo said as they walked over to him. "What are you doing over here?"

"I was walking around listening to everyone wishing for a certain gift, and I suddenly realized I don't know what gift I would want! So I came here to get away from the wishing."

Modo and Jack laughed.

The nervous hum in the hall suddenly quieted when Principal Winkleberry entered.

"Good morning, young magicks!" he said. "As you know, you all possess magickal abilities that are normal for all magicks. In Magick Lab, you are all learning to light your wands, do simple levitation of common objects, and perform some basic disappearing spells—by the way, the missing bat was found in the Hall of Enchantment. As you continue to develop your basic skills, you will also attend classes related to your individual unique gift. So, a few instructions before we begin:

1. Whatever your gift is, embrace it and be happy with it. Your gift wants to work with you, so accept it as your partner in your magick life.

2. You will need to learn how to use your gift. This will take time, patience, and practice. Trust yourself, and trust your gift!

3. While you're enrolled in Lower and Upper Schola, your gift and your magick are only to be used for good. Using your gift for anything other than good can lead to disastrous results for you. Have you seen the jar of broken wands in the front office? Those are wands that had to be destroyed because students tried to use their gift for their own gain. The wands turned on them and they were hit with their own spells.

Then they were expelled from school.

Need I say more?

4. There will be instruction classes for each group of gifts.

Now, let us begin! I'm going to cause something to happen in the middle of the hall. If your gift is related to the occurrence, you will not be able to resist moving toward it."

The students shuffled their feet and began to move together like robots back against the wall. Principal Winkleberry moved to the center of the hall, his yellow bow tie beginning to glow. With a wave of his wand, a large pot filled with dirt appeared. Soon stems and vines began growing from the pot. The sweet smell of carnations filled the air.

"Oh, what is happening?" shouted a girl standing behind Modo. Suddenly, pushing past him, she and three other students ran across the floor and sat by the pot.

"Very good," Principal Winkleberry said. "You are gifted with growing any kind of plant. Congratulations!"

The pot disappeared and the four students were dismissed. Next, a raincloud appeared near the roof of the hall, and rain began to fall onto the floor. Several students began to move toward the cloud, but they didn't run or walk. They danced! Modo and Orrin pointed at the students, shocked to see Jack dancing his way to the center, his little blond head bobbing as he moved. When he arrived, the rain stopped.

"Excellent!" Principal Winkleberry proclaimed. "Your gift is control of the weather through your dancing. Remember, your gift is to be used for good, not for your convenience. Now, off you go, and I don't expect any weather changes today!"

Several more groups were decided, some gifted with cooking and potions, some with building abilities, some with strength and agility. Soon there were only four students remaining, including Orrin and Modo.

"Well," said Principal Winkleberry, "let's see what we have left."

A pad of drawing paper appeared on the floor with a pencil. Principal Winkleberry waved his wand and the pencil began moving across the paper. As the students watched, the pencil drew a dog; then right before their eyes, the dog came to life and walked off the paper, wagging his tail. Orrin and the other two students were on the floor playing with the dog in a matter of seconds.

"Wonderful!" Principal Winkleberry announced. "Your artistic gift will allow you to draw what you need and it will become real. However, it will only remain real for two hours and will then once again be a flat drawing. Enjoy your day and don't draw anything you can't control, my friends."

Orrin and the other artists began to leave.

"But, what about Modo?" Orrin asked. "What is his gift?"

"Modo and I will discuss his gift after you leave. He will be out shortly if you want to wait for him," Principal Winkleberry explained.

Orrin looked at Modo for a second and then left the hall.

Two Gifts?

20

What if I don't want to be a dragon pard?
—MODO JOURNAL ENTRY

"Well, Modo, here we are again—just you and me. What do you think your gift might be?"

"I think it is my music, my flute," Modo answered.

"Yes," Principal Winkleberry replied. "That is one of your gifts. Music is a powerful magick in itself. But your ability to make music brings with it a great responsibility. You can use it to control emotions, Modo—not just yours, but others' also."

"I don't understand," Modo said. "I know how it makes me feel—sometimes it helps calm me down—but how can I control others' emotions?"

"Come with me," Principal Winkleberry said.

Modo followed him out of the Activities Hall and into the Main Office.

"Modo," the principal whispered, turning away from the secretary, "Mrs. Bellefonte is having a bad day. You can cheer her up!"

"How?" Modo asked.

"Choose a piece of happy music and play it for her."

"Okay," Modo said. After thinking a moment, Modo played a jig, music for a fast, rhythmic dance. Mrs. Bellefonte continued adding up numbers on a sheet of paper as Modo played.

"That's nice, dear," Mrs. Bellefonte said, glancing up, and then returning to adding numbers.

Modo looked at Principal Winkleberry and shrugged.

"Now," the principal said, "play it again, and this time, the whole time you are playing, think *happy*. Think only the word happy!"

"Okay," Modo responded. Modo began playing again and thinking *happy, happy, happy!*

Mrs. Bellefonte looked up slowly as a smile crossed her face. Suddenly she stood up, and with a bounce, headed for the door.

"I'll be back, I'm going to lunch. It's a beautiful day!"

Modo watched Mrs. Bellefonte leave and looked at Principal Winkleberry.

"So you see, Modo," Principal Winkleberry said, "you must be very careful with your gift. As with all other gifts, it can only be used for good, not to get what you want for yourself. Do you understand?"

"I think so," Modo whispered, tapping his flute lightly against his leg.

"That is only part of your gift, Modo. You have been chosen by a dragon. That makes you a dragon pard—or you will be one day." Principal Winkleberry walked into his office and motioned for Modo to follow.

"A dragon pard?" Modo asked, sitting down in the chair across from the principal's desk.

"Yes, Modo. There haven't been dragon pards since the dragons disappeared. A dragon chooses a magick to be a companion, an equal. Dragons and their pards work together to protect their communities in times of danger." Principal Winkleberry sat down and watched Modo.

Modo sat quietly for a moment, deep in thought, and then looked up at Principal Winkleberry.

"Do you have a question, Modo?"

"Yes, sir. How did Eboo's egg get here? Did you know he was in there? And why did he pick me?"

"That's three questions, Modo," Principal Winkleberry said, laughing.

"Sorry," Modo murmured, quietly fingering the holes on his flute.

"I'll do my best to explain the arrival of Eboo, but even I don't know everything. Over the Blue Mountains, there is a hidden place called Blooming Grove. It's where the dragons live when they are not needed somewhere in this world. Deep within Blooming Grove lies Lord's Valley, where my great white dragon, Dreyken, resides. When a part of this world becomes too unbalanced, Dreyken sends a dragon to find a pard, and they work together to restore balance."

"So Dreyken sent Eboo. But how did he get here?" Modo asked, glancing at the dragon pendant resting on the principal's chest.

"The Faerie Folk and the dragons have been connected for ages. When Dreyken becomes aware of the need, he calls upon the Faerie Folk to deliver an egg to the area that's out of balance."

"I remember," Modo said, "all the Faerie rings in the woods and around the building the first day of school."

"Yes," Principal Winkleberry affirmed. "Although at certain times the Faerie Folk just like to enjoy themselves, especially in mid-summer! So you can never really know what the Faerie rings mean." Principal Winkleberry chuckled as he shifted in his chair.

"Did you know Eboo's egg was there—which one it was?" Modo asked.

"I noticed the rings, but I didn't know for sure if it meant a dragon egg. I did not know your egg had a dragon in it. Eboo chose you and only he can tell you why. How his egg ended up with his intended pard, I don't know. There is magick everywhere, Modo, more than any of us will ever know or understand."

"Who will teach me how to be a pard?" Modo asked, laying his flute on the desk.

"I will," Principal Winkleberry said, touching the silver dragon pendant. "I am the last remaining dragon pard. At least I was until Eboo chose you. And Modo, Eboo will only respond when you play your flute and call him with your mind. Similar to how you just used your mind in the office. There is one thing I want to tell you. You and Eboo will spend a lot of time together. You may work right here in Anterg to keep the village safe. Other times, as you grow older and more skilled, Dreyken may send you to other places that need help. But there are also times when Dreyken will call Eboo back to Blooming Grove. He may call him back for more dragon training or for reasons only he understands. But be assured, Eboo will come back, and you must use his times away to improve your skills also. No one told me this when Dreyken chose me, and the first time it happened, I was devastated." Principal Winkleberry stood up, turned, and stared out the window.

After a long moment, Modo asked, "Why doesn't Dreyken return, sir?"

"Dreyken is now the Head Dragon, his job is to protect and train the dragons." The principal turned and looked at Modo.

"Sir, will I live 100 years, like you?" Modo squirmed in his seat, not sure what he wanted the answer to be.

"I can't tell you that, Modo. It is different for all dragon pards." Principal Winkleberry paused a moment, then quietly asked, "When Eboo doesn't have to be kept a secret, may I visit with him?"

"Of course, sir, anytime." Modo felt an incredible heaviness descend over him, almost as if Eboo was sitting on his shoulders.

"Don't look so dismayed, Modo. You have been chosen for a great honor, but until we know what danger brought Eboo here, I'm afraid you'll have to keep him a secret a bit longer. The dragons are revered by most folks—naturals and magicks. But they also know a dragon means danger is imminent. We don't want to cause a panic. Unfortunately, there are also people—naturals and magicks—who would try to capture Eboo and use him for their own selfish purposes. So secrecy is the only way, right now, to keep everyone safe. Well, I imagine your friends are waiting for you, so off you go. And Modo, come to me whenever you have questions."

"Thank you, sir, I will." Modo stood, picked up his flute, and slowly left the office.

MUSIC

21

I wish I could talk to Grandma.
—MODO JOURNAL ENTRY

Orrin and Jack were sitting on the stone steps outside
Lower Schola waiting for Modo. The boys were checking
out the covers of their journals, where a new blue crescent
moon had appeared on each—the gifting moon.

"Do you think Modo's gift is music?" Jack asked,
reaching back and returning his journal to his back pocket.

"What else could it be," Orrin replied. "He didn't
react to any of the other gifts."

Modo pushed open the front door of the school and
sat down on the stone steps next to his friends.

"Well?" Orrin asked.

"It's music," Modo said quietly.

"You sound disappointed," Jack said. "At least you
already know how to play. I sure don't know how to

dance!" Jack jumped up and began twirling and twisting around the trees, his arms flapping crazily at his sides. Soon all three boys were jumping, twirling, and spinning. Rolling down the hill in front of the school, the boys landed in a tangled heap by the road.

"We're going over to get a sundae at Scoop-dee-doo," Jack said, laughing as he stood up. "Can you come too?"

"No, but thanks," Modo replied, suddenly serious. "I need to get home."

"Okay, see you later." Jack and Orrin raced away, still laughing and twirling.

Deciding to take a long way home, Modo turned and headed up the curved road past the school. A squirrel scolded him as he passed by an old oak tree, and a blue jay screeched a warning. The animals seemed to feel uneasy around Modo, who they usually welcomed readily. Most days walking the narrow cottage-lined paths of Anterg felt peaceful, but today Modo felt an odd mixture of sadness and fright. A dragon pard. Eboo wasn't just his magickal companion, like Mercedes or Finkle, Modo was his pard; they were equals and would be expected to keep everyone safe. How could he be a dragon pard? He was just a kid!

"Hey, flute boy! Where are you goin'?"

Modo kept walking, in no mood to deal with the older boys.

"Maybe you didn't hear me, flutey boy. Play us a song!"

Modo turned and looked at the older boys. A tall boy with sandy-colored hair stepped toward him.

"Your brother seems to prefer being with his little flute-playing brother lately, rather than us. Why would that be?"

"Yeah," a short, heavyset boy said. "We've seen you guys in the woods. What are you two doin' anyway?"

Modo didn't know if what he was about to do qualified as good, but he was still going to do it.

After pulling his flute from his back pocket, he began playing the spookiest song he knew and thinking *scared*. *Scared, scared, scared*. Modo serenaded the boys and watched as the color drained from their faces, and they turned and ran. *That was good for all of us*, Modo thought and continued home.

As Modo walked up the driveway he saw Mom sitting on the porch. She was slowly rocking in one of the blue rockers. Baskets of pink and white flowers hung along the porch ceiling, and a gentle breeze was shaking a tune from a sea glass wind chime. On the wicker table next to her was a glass pitcher, a plate of cookies, and a large envelope.

Modo climbed the steps to the porch, and Mom smiled at him as Finkle began rubbing up against his legs. Modo

bent down and stroked the orange cat's fur, receiving loud purring approval.

"Come sit with me," she said. "How was the gift giving?"

"Fine," Modo replied. "Orrin can draw things to life and Jack can dance the weather."

"And you?" Mom said gently, offering Modo a molasses cookie.

"My gift is my music. And—" Modo couldn't say it out loud.

"And you are a dragon pard."

He looked at his mother, remembering when he could sit on her lap and be comforted. He longed for that comfort now, but he sat down in the other rocker. Finkle jumped up in his lap and began kneading his shirt with her paws.

"Modo," Mom said. "I have something that might help." She handed him the large envelope. It was heavy with a dark stain on one side and smelled damp and musty. "Go on, open it."

Modo handed Finkle over to Mom, opened the end of the envelope, and pulled out a stack of papers. Turning over the first sheet, he saw that it was flute music. There was old music by the Masters, folk tunes, and music charts known as jazz.

"Modo," Mom said. "Your grandmother's gift was also music. I've been saving her music for you ever since you started playing her flute. I remember her saying that knowing different kinds of music helped her use her gift in different situations. She would be so pleased with your playing, and so proud. Like your father and I are."

"But, Mom," Modo began. "A dragon pard?"

"Don't worry about being a dragon pard right now. You have time to learn. Eboo will help you."

Mom reached over and pulled out a piece of music.

"Here," she said. "Grandma had two copies of this one. Check out the writing at the bottom of the page."

Modo looked closely at the faint handwritten words: *A Call.*

"Was Grandma a pard?" Modo asked, somehow comforted by that idea.

"I don't think so," Mom answered. "Unless she was before she met Grandpa. When she died, we found a note saying that it was important that whoever showed a love for playing her flute must learn this piece of music. That's why I hung it in your bedroom."

"Did the note say anything else?" Modo asked, leaning back in the rocker.

"There was a strange sentence about how hard it is to be torn by two great loves. I don't know what that means," Mom said. "I do know she stopped playing her flute when she met Grandpa. Anyway, would you play it for me?"

Smiling, Modo pulled out his flute and quietly began playing "A Dragon's Wish," being careful not to call Eboo in his mind. Mom leaned back in her rocker, closed her eyes, and became lost in the music.

Practicing Gifts

...and I'm still growing things.
—GAVIN JOURNAL ENTRY

Orrin, Jack, and Modo were waiting for Gavin in the parking shed. Their school gifting lessons hadn't begun yet, so Gavin offered to help them practice. The faded red double doors were open to the tree-lined driveway where dappled sun spots covered the ground. Inside the shed, the boys sat around on the old green moving pads, drinking lemonade and eating cookies.

The back screen door slammed and Gavin walked in carrying a pot of marigolds from the back porch.

"Watch this," he said. He laid his hand on one yellow flower and instantly it began to grow. Normally the size of a Ping-Pong ball, it was soon as big as a basketball.

"Wow!" the boys exclaimed. "That's amazing!"

"Did it take long to learn how to do it?" Orrin asked.

"Well," Gavin said, "that's only a little flower. It will be a while before I can change a big bush or a tree. The trick is to keep trying."

"Will it stay that big?" Jack asked.

"It will if it's taken care of properly," Gavin replied. "Not sure Mom would want a giant marigold, so I'll change it back to normal size." *Normal*, Gavin thought. Not nearly as exciting as a dragon. Tapping the flower, he shrank it back to its original size. "Okay, Orrin, let's see what you can do."

Orrin laid a pad of paper in his lap. Slowly he drew a spider, an ant, and a lizard. Nothing happened.

"Now what?" Orrin asked, looking up at Gavin.

"Well, eventually you will be able to just think them alive, but in the beginning, you probably need to think your magick word, touch them, and say 'Alive.'"

Orrin glanced at the other boys, reached his hand out, paused a second and, touching the spider, whispered "Alive." Instantly the spider scurried off the paper and into a dark corner of the shed, heading for one of the many webs along the walls.

"Woo-hoo!" Orrin shouted. He touched the ant and lizard to life, and Orrin and the other boys fist-pumped and laughed.

"Your turn, Jack," Gavin said.

"I'm a little embarrassed," Jack said. "Controlling the weather is cool, but the dancing part, well, not so much."

"When you think about it," Gavin said, "the weather usually involves motion—wind blowing, rain and snow falling, temperatures climbing and diving. One boy last year had the same gift, but he could never make thunder. He would dance every dance he could think of, but no thunder. One day, out of frustration, he started doing back flips in the middle of his dancing. Every time he flipped, there was a *boom*! He was so excited we finally had to grab him. The thunder was shaking the building. Dancing makes sense! You have a neat gift, Jack."

"I guess so," Jack said, "but it still feels weird. What shall I do, maybe a few snowflakes?"

"Sure, just not a blizzard!" Orrin grinned and picked up his drawing pad to make room for Jack's weather.

Jack stood in the middle of the parking shed. He closed his eyes and thought snow and cold. Slowly, as his mind went over to the snow, his arms floated upward over his head and he silently began spinning across the floor. One small, white flake fell from his fingers. Soon more and more floated all around him. Gently and magically a small pile of snow built up around his feet.

"I guess we're going to have to call him Jack Frost," Orrin said, laughing. The boys began making snowballs and throwing them at Jack, who stopped dancing and opened his eyes.

"Pretty cool, Jack—really *cool*, if you know what I mean," Orrin said.

"Wow," Jack said. "Makes you a bit tired, doesn't it?"

"Yeah," Gavin said. "You'll learn in your classes how to know when you must stop. Doing magick for too long can totally exhaust you. And, Jack, you'll have to keep your eyes open."

"Modo's turn," Jack and Orrin said together.

Gavin looked at Modo and winked.

"Actually," Gavin said, "you've heard Modo play his flute."

"Yeah, but what happens when he plays it, you know, magickally?" Jack asked.

"Well," Modo said, "let me show you."

Modo began playing a slow, dreary song thinking *sad. Sad, sad, sad.* One by one, Gavin, Jack, and Orrin became still. Gavin slowly sat down and in a moment his head was hanging down. Orrin slid to the floor and curled up in a ball on a moving pad. Jack was quietly crying. Modo stopped playing and waited. In a few moments the boys looked up.

"That was so sad," Gavin said. "Can you only make us sad?"

Modo picked up his flute and began playing the jig he played for Mrs. Bellefonte, thinking *happy. Happy, happy, happy.*

Within seconds, the boys were looking up, then standing up and laughing. Soon they were dancing around the parking shed, swatting at spiderwebs, and raising clouds of dust.

Modo stopped playing and grinned.

"Wow," Orrin said. "Imagine how you could control people!"

"I can only use it for good. Remember?" Modo replied.

"Yeah, well," Orrin said with a shrug, "there is that."

Flying North

23

Eboo was beginning to look more like a grown dragon. His wings were too large to open in the cave, and his scales were turning from brown to a rich beautiful green that sparkled when hit by the sun. His snout was much longer, with faint puffs of steam sometimes rising over his head. The spikes on Eboo's back were hardening into protective plates with the ones on the base of his neck forming a natural seat for a rider. Eboo was becoming restless and bored. Every night he flew south from Old Turtle Pond, over the Blue Mountains, and hunted in the game lands. But tonight, with no moon, he decided to fly north over the farmlands. He would not hunt to eat. He would hunt something else. Hopefully, Modo's father would not be angry!

Eboo rose over the pond and, skimming the trees, flew around Anterg, continuing over the wooded hills that sheltered the village. A short time later, the hills dropped away to quilted farm fields bordered by dark tree lines. An occasional lone tree stood sentry in the middle of a field or meadow.

Eboos's keen eyesight saw owls swooping toward field mice and voles. A young coyote trotted through a cut cornfield, heading toward a creek. Many fields were dotted with cows and sheep grazing or sleeping. Eboo's silent flight went unnoticed.

Staying away from lighted areas, Eboo flew closer and closer to Nonabel. At first, the smell was faint, a slight change in the air. But as Eboo approached the outskirts of Nonabel, the unmistakable smell of cucumbers filled his snout. Repelled by the noxious odor, Eboo banked sharply to the left and headed home to Modo and Anterg.

NONABEL

24

*I hope Dreyken never calls Eboo back
to Blooming Grove.*
—MODO JOURNAL ENTRY

"Dad," Modo yelled, running into the house on Saturday morning. "Dad, Eboo isn't in his cave, and he's always back by now!"

"Slow down, Modo. C'mon, I'll go back with you. But we're walking—running will call attention to us."

Modo and Father headed down the hill toward the village, the air feeling crisper and cooler as autumn approached. The smell of wood smoke drifted on the breeze. A few brown leaves drifted down, and other trees had begun to show their autumn attire. Squirrels and chipmunks scampered busily across the path, carrying acorns to their winter hideouts. Several Faerie rings shone in the sunlight that reached the forest floor.

Entering the village, they stopped at the small grocery store, checked for letters at the Mail Station, and chatted with friends at Scoop-dee-doo. Moving slowly in the shadows across the street, Tommy stooped to pick up a rock as he followed them.

As they left the village, Father hesitated. "It feels like we're being watched," he said quietly. "You go ahead, Modo. I'll stay here and look around." Modo learned very young that his father's gift was sensing who or what was around him, even if they weren't visible. No matter how hard he and Gavin tried to sneak up on him, Father always caught them.

Modo turned down the dirt path to Old Turtle Pond, moving under the leaves on the maple trees that formed a yellow-and-red tunnel leading to the pond. In the bright daylight, he noticed that the bushes around the mouth of the cave were beginning to be broken and smashed by Eboo's expanding wings. Modo looked around and slipped into the cave.

Father stood quietly by the road, watching, waiting, and sensing. Then he saw him: Tommy slowly walking in the shadows under the trees.

Father stepped out into the road and greeted the boy.

"Hi, Tommy," he said. "We haven't seen you in a while. How are you?"

"Ah, fine," Tommy stammered, digging the toe of his shoe into the dirt.

"What are you doing over this way?" Father asked, idly picking up a twig and breaking it into little pieces.

"Over this way? Oh, looking for rocks for my collection," Tommy answered. His eyes darted from side to side.

"So you're still building rock animals?"

"Yeah," Tommy said. "Where's Modo? Is he with you?"

"Not right now," Father answered. "Well, I hope we get to see you more often."

"Yeah, me too," Tommy said. Then he slowly moved across the road and headed back into the village, glancing back toward Father several times.

"Whew," Modo said to Eboo. "You're back. I was worried. Father is keeping watch. He thought we were being followed."

"Go get Father, bring him quick. Tell him Eboo knows the trick."

Modo ran out of the cave, hurried past the well and around the pond, bending under low-hanging limbs and slipping on the muddy pond edge. When he saw the main road, he slowed to a walk and then hid behind a thorn bush. At the end of the path, Father was talking to Tommy. Was Tommy following him?

Modo waited, hardly breathing until Tommy turned and headed back into the village. He waited a few more minutes and walked over to Father. The noisy birds were now quiet as a gentle breeze blew through the trees, rustling the leaves with messages and gossip.

"Dad, was Tommy following us?" Modo asked.

"I think so," Father answered. "He acted very nervous and kept looking around. I'm not sure what he wanted, but I sensed something was wrong. Is Eboo back?"

"Yes," Modo said. "He needs you to come to the cave right away."

Father turned in each direction, checking that Tommy was truly gone, and they hurried back through the maple tree tunnel to the cave.

"Hello, Eboo. Boy, you sure have grown! Do you have something to tell me?" Father asked.

"Eboo flies very late, following Gorlings' smell of hate. In the place called Nonabel, that is where the Gorlings dwell."

"Nonabel. Hiding in the city," Father said. "I trust you didn't hunt, that you were only scouting."

"Eboo hunts only south, no cows or chickens in his mouth."

Father smiled. "His rhyming cracks me up sometimes." Becoming more serious, Father continued, "We will have to alert the magick community. We can't keep this a secret any longer. Good work, Eboo. C'mon, Modo, we better get going."

Modo reached up and stroked Eboo's snout. "I'll play the flute for him a little and then I'll come home. Is that all right?"

"Just be careful, especially coming into the village. I'll send Gavin over to grow more stems on the bushes around the cave. You can stay here and wait for him."

"Okay, Dad. Thanks!"

Eboo was already humming when Father left the cave.

CAUGHT

25

I feel like a traitor,
a snitch.
—TOMMY JOURNAL ENTRY

Tommy knew Julian was watching him. He could feel his eyes on him as he walked to and from school, collected rocks, and built rock animals. Tommy had a pile of rocks behind his house and a small area where he worked. Most evenings, he searched for rocks to add to his collection—rocks that could be bodies, heads, tails, or legs. Tommy's animals were scattered throughout his mother's gardens.

When Tommy was building his rock animals, he felt a sense of peacefulness. The rough surfaces of some rocks and the smooth glass sides of others helped his mind relax. He loved stacking them up to form cats, birds, elephants, whatever the rocks told him to build.

Tommy lived on the edge of Anterg, with a stretch of shrubs and bushes between the yard and the woods. Hearing a breaking twig, Tommy looked up.

"Tommy, what are you doing?" It was Julian, his voice floating out of the bushes.

"I like to create animals with the rocks. They become friends. I talk to them."

Poking his head out of the bushes, Julian asked, "You sure you aren't a magick?"

"I'm sure. Someday I would like to be a sculptor like in the book Modo gave me, and make animals for gardens. Someday..." Tommy picked up a flat rock and began to balance it on four small stones.

"I saw you following Modo and his father. What did you find out?" Julian whispered, leaning further out of the bush.

"I'm not sure. Modo's father stopped me at the path to Old Turtle Pond. He asked me about school and my rocks, but I think he knew I was following them. I didn't get to talk to Modo. How can I turn against my friend? I don't know what to do! I don't want to hurt him!"

"She will enslave you if you don't do what she asks. I'll never be free because I tried to run away. Find out what she wants, and maybe she will let you go because you are young." Julian's shoulders were emerging from the shrub.

"And maybe I'll never be free, either," Tommy said, adding a round stone at one end of the flat rock.

"Warneke won't wait long for our return. Let's hide near Old Turtle Pond this evening and see if Modo comes. You walk every evening hunting rocks anyway, so it won't seem unusual," Julian said, falling out of the bush and landing on his hands and knees.

It was dusk when Modo reached the path to Old Turtle Pond. He looked in every direction before heading under the patchwork of red and yellow leaves, worried now that someone was watching him. As he approached the pond, he heard the bullfrogs beginning their evening songs while cooling off in the pond mud. A gentle breeze spun the leaves on the poplar trees and glints of gold flashed in the water as the coy fish swam just below the surface. Modo was amazed at the new vines and bushes Gavin had grown to disguise the cave. He almost missed the entrance.

"Hi, Eboo. Are you about ready to go hunting?" Modo asked.

"Eboo is ready to hunt a deer, but Eboo feels someone is near."

"Someone near here? Maybe Father was right, and someone is watching us. Go quickly, Eboo, go and hunt. I'll slip away after you're gone."

Modo listened as Eboo's wings whooshed him into the night sky, over the pond and away from the cave.

"Now what do I do?" Modo asked, his voice echoing in the empty cave as he paced throughout the rock room.

"You could introduce me to your dragon," Tommy said quietly from the mouth of the cave. He was only a silhouette against the evening light reflecting off the pond.

Modo spun around, his glasses slipping down his nose.

"Tommy, you *have* been following me! Why? Why couldn't you just stay away?" Modo cried.

"I just couldn't. Modo, the dragon is incredible and beautiful, but now you must be careful, very careful. And…and I'm sorry." Tommy ran from the cave, tears blinding his vision as he pushed through the bushes to where Julian was waiting.

THE SECRET IS OUT

I'm a failure.
—MODO JOURNAL ENTRY

Modo raced after Tommy, hoping to catch him and swear him to secrecy. But Tommy was nowhere to be seen; all Modo saw was a roadster passing the entrance of the path to the pond.

Modo returned to the cave and paced across the floor. He kicked at Eboo's hay pile, then plopped down on a sleeping bag. Should he tell Father or maybe Gavin? Or should he keep trying to find Tommy and swear him to secrecy? Eboo wouldn't return until morning, so there was nothing to do but go home.

Modo slowed his breathing, remembering Father's advice to move slowly and not draw attention to himself. But as he walked slowly, his eyes darted from side to side, looking for any sign of Tommy. He checked the Village

Store, the Mail Station, and Scoop-dee-doo. But Tommy had disappeared.

Modo trudged home, not even aware of where he was, just moving slowly through the narrow paths between the cottages. Up above, Mercedes flew, keeping watch over the boy.

Father and Gavin were outside practicing wandless fireworks when Modo walked up the driveway.

"Why the gloomy look?" Father asked as Modo came into the yard.

Looking down, Modo shuffled from side to side, afraid to speak. Gavin was teasing Finkle, setting off sparkling whizzers over the cat's head, just out of reach.

"Modo," Father said. "What is it? Is Eboo all right?"

"Tommy," Modo whispered, pushing his glasses up.

"Tommy?" asked Gavin, trying to stop the smoke pouring out of his wand. "What about Tommy?"

"He found the cave. He was following us. He saw Eboo." Modo's voice quivered.

"Where is Tommy now?" Father asked, leaning over and tapping Gavin's wand. The smoke curled into the air and was gone.

"I don't know, he ran away. He told me to be careful and that he was sorry."

"Why would he say sorry? Tommy might be in trouble," Father said. "Let's go inside. I must call the Magick Council to order right away. Eboo will have to be moved. Gavin, start thinking right now of a new place. You and Modo, go look for Tommy, but don't be obvious about it."

"Dad," Modo said. "I'm scared. What if the Gorlings go after Tommy? Eboo and I don't know what to do or how to fight them."

"If it comes to that, Modo, you will do what you must. Maybe Eboo came now because of the Gorlings, or maybe there is another reason we don't know yet."

Modo stood quietly. When he looked up at Gavin, he saw a worried look cross his face before he smiled at his little brother.

"Let's go," Gavin said. "Can you grab Finkle and put her in the house? She won't let me near her!"

Modo picked up the orange cat, put her in the house, and then ran to catch up with Gavin. He had failed Eboo. He hadn't kept the secret. He hadn't kept Eboo safe.

THE MAGICK COUNCIL

Father stepped off the porch and headed down the narrow walkway in the soft light of dusk. A few porch lanterns were lit, but tonight he didn't enjoy their friendly light as he walked to the Hall of Enchantment. He was pensive, realizing he was about to change the lives of the villagers by revealing Eboo's presence and the dragon's revelation about the Gorlings.

The Hall of Enchantment was a large building nestled in tall pines near the Scoop-dee-doo. Many times the council met on the wide yellow-and-green covered porch, attending to matters such as schools, projects with the naturals, and any issues brought forth by the community. As Father approached the hall, he noticed the shadows cast by the colorful glass lanterns were only of empty rocking chairs. He had requested that the meeting be held inside, behind closed doors.

"What's going on, Malarkey?" asked Dunmore Throop, the head of the council, as Father entered the room. "Why are we meeting at an unscheduled time and not on the porch?" Father closed the door, moved to the center of the room, and stood by a large wooden table.

The Hall of Enchantment had been the home of the Magick Council for centuries. Its narrow pine-board walls had darkened over time. The tall windows allowed in any light that filtered through the towering pine trees.

Father looked around the table. Dunmore sat at one end looking mad at the world. Next to Dunmore was Orrin's dad, Michael. Three more members sat on the other side of the table. Margarite Moonstone was the Headmistress of Second School, and Jack's mother, Freya, sat next to her. The third, Isla Newton, worked in the Village Store and represented the magicks on the Community Council.

Father cleared his throat and quietly said, "When my son, Modo, tested for Lower Schola, he was chosen by a dragon."

"Excuse me," Orrin's dad said. "Did you say a dragon? A real dragon right here in Anterg?"

Jack's mother sat up, her eyes wide, her mouth open in amazement. "A dragon," she whispered dreamily.

"Yes," Father said. "A beautiful, amazing dragon. We've kept him hidden. When he began flying, we moved him to a secluded spot. Obviously, I'm asking that you keep our secret until we know why the dragon is here."

"Are you sure you can keep him hidden?" Dunmore Throop asked.

"We are now, but he was seen by a young natural so we are moving him again. We think the boy, Tommy Aldan, may be in trouble. But that is only part of the

reason I called for this meeting. The dragon flew to the Watchtower and Nonabel and smelled Gorlings."

"Gorlings!" Everyone moved at once, knocking over their wooden chairs as they jumped up shouting.

"That can't be, Warneke was defeated long ago!"

"The dragon is young, maybe it doesn't know what it's smelling."

"This can't be, it just can't!"

"Silence!" Dunmore shouted. "The Gorlings almost took control of our village once before. Using the power of their music and art, they tried to destroy us. We can't pretend this isn't true. We also can't overreact. Malarkey, keep me informed, especially if the dragon brings you any more information. Isla, keep an eye out—if Tommy comes in the store, find out if he's all right. I will travel to Nonabel and see if I can find out anything about the Gorlings, where they are hiding. Be vigilant, and report anything suspicious!"

Everyone sat quietly for a moment, all lost in their own thoughts.

"Has the boy been able to call the dragon yet?" Dunmore asked.

"He's called him once, but he has no training in mind talk. I don't know if he could call him again," Father replied.

"How did he call him, what is his gift?" Dunmore inquired, nervously tapping his fingers on the table.

"He plays the flute," Father replied.

"Then we must quietly advise our gifted musicians to be ready, in case we are dealing with Warneke again. Without them, we can't defeat her. Also, alert the artists and builders, as it could be a Gorling other than Warneke who is near. We'll meet again soon. Are we all in agreement?"

Six knuckles hit the table together. *Tap-tap, tap-tap-tap.*

The colorful lanterns went out one by one as the magicks silently stepped off the porch and left the Hall of Enchantment. Somehow the night seemed darker now.

RETURN TO NONABEL

Is there such a thing as a good lie?
—TOMMY JOURNAL ENTRY

Tommy looked out his bedroom window, watching his mom filling the bird feeders. He never lied to his mom, but now he was going to so he could go back to Warneke. If he didn't go, Warneke would hunt him down and then hurt not only him and Julian, but his mom too.

Tommy joined his mom behind the house filling the bird feeders and putting out corn for the deer and squirrels. After Tommy's dad died, his mom found comfort in taking care of the birds and other critters that shared Anterg with the naturals and magicks.

Picking up a bag of sunflower seeds, Tommy headed to an empty feeder near his mom.

"Thanks," Mom said. "These guys are really chowing down—getting ready for the cold weather, I guess.

"Could I stay over at Chris's house? We have to work on our nature study," Tommy said. "It's complicated, so if Chris and I can work late it would really help."

"I'll have to see Chris's mom and make sure it's okay," she replied, spreading cracked corn on a large flat rock.

"Oh, I forgot." Tommy reached into his back pocket and pulled a folded paper from his journal. "Here's a note Chris gave me in school from his mom explaining it all."

Tommy's mom unfolded the note and read it slowly.

"Well, it looks all right," she said. "But be back early in the morning—we have chores to do, remember? Raking the leaves, planting more spring bulbs?" Mom turned to put suet in the basket hanging on a tree trunk.

"Okay," Tommy said. "Thanks. I love you, Mom."

Tommy's mom was surprised, but pleased, when he unexpectedly hugged her.

Later, Tommy met Julian at the edge of the village. Checking that no one was watching, Tommy jumped into Julian's roadster, and they headed for Nonabel.

Warneke, wrapped in a dark green cape, stood at the tall windows of her brick house, smiling as Julian pulled up. She watched Tommy climb out of the roadster and slowly walk up to the door. Stopping several times to look at the jungle of bright flowers lining the walkway, he seemed to be listening for something.

Warneke opened the door, glared at Tommy, and with a creepy, toothy grin spreading across her face, turned and entered the house. Tommy and Julian followed her down the dark hallway to the large living room.

"You're back, and in good time. You have something to tell me?" she asked.

"Maybe," Tommy said.

"Maybe?" Warneke said. "What does that mean?"

Tommy pulled himself up as tall as he could. "Maybe I don't want to betray my friend when I don't know what your plans are," he declared.

"Right now," Warneke said, picking up her violin, "*this* is my plan!"

Launching into a horrible, shrieking song, she punished Tommy repeatedly with screeching runs that grew louder and faster. The music stabbed Tommy's mind, the pain moving in waves over his brain. He rolled in agony on the floor, his body jerking as if being hit by bolts of lightning. Warneke seemed unable to stop, playing on and on and on. Suddenly, Julian threw himself over Tommy screaming, "Mistress, stop! Stop, you'll kill him!"

Warneke slowly shook her head, her eyes staring blankly at nothing, and then laid down the violin.

Tommy lay quivering on the floor. Acid bile filled his mouth, and he fought the urge to throw up. Warneke got down beside him and whispered, "Where is the dragon?"

"In a cave hidden behind Old Turtle Pond, at the edge of Anterg," Tommy said, sobbing.

Warneke stood up. "Now, to capture the boy and the dragon before they can ruin my plans. And you, Tommy, will be the bait."

Warneke bounced out of the room, ignoring her violin.

EBOO MOVES

29

I don't like this,
I NEED to see Eboo every day!
—MODO JOURNAL ENTRY

Modo looked for Tommy before and after school, but he couldn't find him. He finally headed home to meet Father and Gavin to move Eboo once again. The treetops swayed back and forth, appearing to be looking for Tommy too.

"Any sign of him?" Father asked when Modo came into the kitchen, letting the screen door slam.

"No, nowhere," Modo answered, grabbing the lemonade pitcher from the cold cupboard and pouring himself a glass full.

"Okay. Well, let's figure out where Eboo is going, and then we'll look for Tommy."

Modo finished his drink and ran upstairs to get Gavin. A few minutes later, they headed down the hill, through the village to Old Turtle Pond. When Father was sure they weren't being followed, they headed down the dirt path to the pond and the cave. A floating blanket of fallen leaves on the surface of the pond was accented by the golden koi fish swimming below. The distant drumming of a woodpecker interrupted the stillness. Modo circled around the well and disappeared through the thicket.

Modo gently nudged Eboo's snout. "Wake up, Eboo. You have to move again."

"Eboo likes this secret place, it is a very comfy space. Why must Eboo go away? Doesn't Modo want Eboo to stay?"

"Eboo, of course I want you to stay. But when you left the last time, my friend Tommy saw you. Now we're afraid you aren't safe here."

"Eboo can fight, Eboo has might! Nothing is dire when Eboo has fire!"

Eboo stood up, took a deep, deep breath, and blew with all his might. A wisp of smoke and a single small spark escaped from his snout.

Modo giggled, stood up, and patted Eboo's neck.

"I think it's better to move you," he said. "Do you have any ideas where you could go?"

"Eboo doesn't like this plan, but he will try to understand. Up near the Watchtower, there are rocks and trees; Eboo can hide and no one sees."

Eboo followed Modo out of the cave and listened while Modo explained Eboo's idea to Father and Gavin.

"The only problem," Modo said, "is how will I see Eboo?"

"We will meet at the cave every other night, after dark," Father said. "I will come with you, and we will make sure

Eboo is okay. And Eboo, you keep an eye out for anything out of the ordinary, especially if you fly near Nonabel again."

"*Eboo will fly very, very high, stay out of sight and meet every other night.*"

"Be careful, Eboo," Modo said, stroking his neck. "I'll see you soon."

"*Play the Call before Eboo goes, so that Eboo will really know; Modo will come another day, a day when Eboo can always stay.*"

Father and Gavin headed out to the main road to wait for Modo. Pulling out his wooden flute, Modo sat down, leaned against Eboo's side, and began to play. Over and over he played the rising melody that ended in a gentle descent until he felt Eboo humming.

"Goodbye, Eboo," he whispered.

Missing

Dad doesn't get it—he doesn't understand!
—Modo journal entry

The next day, Modo went to Tommy's house hoping he would be there.

"I'm sorry, Modo," Tommy's mom said. "He was at Chris's house overnight working on their nature study. I know he would like to see you."

"Thanks, maybe I'll run over there and see them," Modo answered.

He walked the three blocks to Chris's house, which sat at the quiet end of a hilltop street that stopped at the woods. Bright red cardinals flitted through the trees as squirrels scampered up the trunks, tails curling and flicking. At the bottom of the hill, the creek from Old Turtle Pond wandered through the forest, diamonds of reflected sunlight twinkling through the tree branches.

Modo skipped up the steps, crossed the narrow porch, and knocked on the carved wooden door.

"Hey, Modo," Chris said when he answered the door. "Miss you at school."

"Hi, Chris," Modo said. "Is Tommy here?"

"Tommy? Why would Tommy be here?"

Modo felt a sick feeling in his stomach, a swirling storm spinning his insides.

"Isn't he here working on your nature study?"

"Nature study? We don't do those until next month! What are you talking about?"

"I guess I misunderstood. Sorry to bother you." Modo turned to leave.

"Hey, don't you want to hang out for a while?" Chris asked.

"Some other time. Right now I have to get home—quick."

Modo ran the whole way home and dashed into the house, screen door slamming as he yelled, "Dad, Dad! Tommy is missing!"

"Slow down, Modo, what's going on? How do you know?"

"I talked to his mom; she said he was overnight at Chris's working on a nature study. But he's not there, and Chris didn't know what I was talking about! He's missing, Dad. What are we going to do? Where could he be?"

Modo was pacing the kitchen floor so fast the pots and pans were rattling in the cupboards. Finkle ran from the room, sliding around the corner into the hallway.

Mercedes, sitting on the porch railing, began flapping his wings and caw-cawing.

Father stepped across the room and grabbed Modo's shoulders, turning him so they were facing each other.

"Modo, stop! Slow down, your brain won't work when you're panicked. If you want to help Tommy, you must stay calm, breathe, and let your mind work."

Modo took a deep breath and tried to stand still. But his heart kept racing, rushing in his ears, fluttering in his chest.

"The magick community is already looking for him," Father said. "Meanwhile, we'll meet Eboo and see if he's noticed anything."

"Maybe I just misunderstood."

Missing Two

31

I'm losing everyone. I'm scared.
What is happening??
—Modo journal entry

Modo, Gavin, and Father headed to Old Turtle Pond. Although they were still careful, Father felt sure no one was watching them.

Modo ran ahead when they reached the dirt path, the moon lighting his way. A strong breeze was beginning to blow as he headed down the tree tunnel to the pond. The leaves on the trees were blowing away from him, their light undersides making him feel unwelcome. Ignoring the leaves, Modo hurried around the pond and past the well, eager to see Eboo after two days without him. It was the longest Eboo and Modo had been apart since the first day of school.

Pushing through the prickly branches covering the cave mouth, Modo called out, "Eboo, we're here!"

Modo stopped abruptly. The cave was empty. Father and Gavin entered the cave, lit their wands, and looked around.

"He's not here," Modo whispered.

"We'll wait a little while," Father replied.

Modo slumped down in the hay, watching Gavin walk around pretending to examine the water markings on the cave walls. Father went back outside and sat in the moonlight by the well.

Ten minutes became fifteen, fifteen became twenty, then twenty became thirty. Gavin left his wand with Modo and went outside to wait with Father. Modo pulled his flute out of his back pocket and quietly played some old folk songs. The soft melodies floated through the cave, quietly clinging to the walls and fading away into the stone. He wanted to call Eboo with his mind and music, but that was only for emergencies. And even though this felt like an emergency, Modo knew it wasn't. Not yet.

After an hour, Father came back into the cave.

"It's time to go home, Modo. I don't think he's coming," Father said gently. "You head home with Gavin, I'll stop and tell Dunmore he didn't come back.

"I think he's mad about the move. He didn't really want to go," Modo said, standing up.

"I doubt that is the reason," Father said. "I'm sure Eboo will explain when he returns."

"But what if he's hurt or captured or something? He may need our help, we can't just abandon him!" Modo shouted.

"Modo!" Father said sternly.

"I know, I know—stay calm, breathe, think. I'm trying, I'm trying. But one of my best friends and my dragon are both missing!"

Modo ran from the cave, pushed past Gavin, and headed toward the village, leaves scattering behind him as he ran.

SETTING THE TRAP

32

I promised Dad I'd take care of Mom!
—TOMMY JOURNAL ENTRY

"I need to go home first," Tommy said to Julian as they drove from Nonabel to Anterg. "My mom needs to see me so she doesn't get suspicious, and I need to keep her from going to Chris's house."

Julian turned onto the winding road leading to Anterg. The trees became thicker as they approached the village, creating a green corridor over the road, drawing naturals and magicks home.

While Julian drove straight through the village, Tommy slid low in his seat, staying hidden from view. Julian pulled into Racket Park, across the road from Hocus Pocus Lake, a favorite swimming spot for the citizens of Anterg.

"I'll be back in a couple of hours," Tommy said, grabbing the side handle.

"Why so long?" Julian asked.

"I can't rush in and out, Mom would be suspicious. I'll think of a way to get out again. Anyway, Modo doesn't go to the cave until evening."

"See you in a few hours," Julian said. "And Tommy, make sure you come back. Remember, if you tell anyone, Warneke will hurt not only you and me, but your mother too."

"I know," Tommy replied. "I'll be back, I promise."

Tommy slipped out of the roadster and headed home, trying to appear normal. He walked up one of the cottage-lined paths, keeping away from the main road through the village. He had to figure out a plan, or this might be his last walk through the stillness of Anterg.

He hated lying to his mom, but he didn't know what else to do, so he was going to do it again.

"Hi, Mom," Tommy called as he came in the house, letting the screen door slap shut behind him.

"There you are," Mom replied. "I'm in the kitchen. I was just getting ready to walk to Chris's house. You were supposed to be home early, remember?"

"Oh, yeah. Guess I forgot, sorry." Tommy sat down on a kitchen stool, picked out an apple from the fruit bowl, and took a bite.

"How's the nature study going? Did Modo like it?" Mother asked.

"Modo? Ah, yeah, he thought it was pretty cool," Tommy stammered, taking another bite.

"Well, I'm glad you got to see each other again."

"Yeah, it was good. How about some lunch, Mom? I'm starving."

"As usual," Mom said, smiling.

After turkey sandwiches and sweet tea, Tommy and his mom began raking leaves.

"Ah, Mom," Tommy said, "you haven't been to see Aunt Susan in a while. If you wanted to go visit her, I'm sure I could stay at Chris's house. I bet she would love to see you." Tommy raked a pile of leaves into a large bag.

"She would," Mom said, "and I'd love to see her. But now isn't a good time for me to go—too much to do at work, and getting the house ready for winter."

"Well, maybe just for a weekend?" Tommy asked, picking up his rake.

Mom looked at Tommy, started to ask a question, and then stopped. "Not now, Tommy, but it's nice of you to think of it."

After finishing the raking, Tommy sat down near his rock pile in the backyard. He thought about running away, but Julian's experience convinced him that the consequences were too severe for him to risk it. He had to protect his mother, but he also needed to warn Modo. He sat with his head in his hands, staring at the rock pile. How did he get in this mess? Lying to his mother, riding to Nonabel with a stranger, helping capture Modo. What was happening to him? There had to be a way out of this, but he was running out of time. And he was scared for his mother.

Tommy picked out a white stone with smooth rounded edges from an old wooden box where he kept his favorite pieces. He had found the quartz on a beach several years ago when he was little and his father took him to see The Big Water. Tommy began to scratch lines on one of his rocks with the quartz. When he was small, he used to draw pictures on flat rocks as presents for his mother.

Draw pictures on rocks? Tommy quickly began putting rocks in his bag and stuck the quartz in his pocket. He had a plan.

"I'll be back later, Mom. I saw some cool rocks in the village last week. I'd like to go check them out." Tommy picked up his canvas rock bag and headed for the door.

"Okay," Mom replied. "But be back before dark."

"Will do," Tommy said as he walked out the door, carrying his bag of rocks. At the end of the driveway, Tommy carefully piled up several rocks, with a flat one on the top. Pulling out the quartz, he drew on the rock and then walked on toward the village. Reaching the corner, Tommy stopped again, took more rocks out of his bag, piled them up, and wrote on the top one. He repeated this several times until he was close to the edge of the village, where he placed one last pile.

Then he ran back to the roadster at Racket Park as fast as he could and slipped into the front seat next to Julian.

Julian looked at Tommy. "Warneke will meet us at the cave to wait for Modo's nightly visit. Are you ready?"

"Ready," Tommy replied.

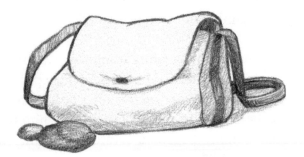

TURTLES

Anterg was not still. Rushing down from the slopes of the Blue Mountains, a strong wind bent the treetops, pushing them toward the ground. The constant murmur of the wood winds became a backdrop to the normal song of Anterg.

Modo decided to check Tommy's house one more time, hoping he had come home. Father sent Mercedes along, in case Modo ran into trouble.

Walking up to the front porch, Modo smiled at the red hummingbird feeders, knowing they would soon come down as the hummers headed to warmer winter homes. Little chickadees dove in and out of a feeder swinging in the wind as blue-gray nuthatches moved headfirst down the trunks searching for bugs in the bark crevices. *At least some things still seem normal*, he thought.

But as Modo knocked on the door, the swirling stomach storm returned. Mercedes ruffled his feathers and resettled on a branch away from the feeders.

"Hello, Modo," Tommy's mom said when she answered the door. "I don't believe it, you just missed Tommy. Wow, it's getting windy!"

"He's been home?" Modo said hopefully.

"Well, of course," answered Tommy's mom.

"Where did he go?" Modo asked.

"He said there were some rocks he wanted to check out. I'm sure you can find him if you look around the village."

"Thanks," Modo replied. Waving to Mercedes, he headed down the porch steps. As he got to the end of Tommy's short driveway, Modo saw a pile of rocks. Looking closer, he realized it was a turtle. Modo started walking home, but Mercedes began squawking, flying straight to the turtle. Modo came back—Mercedes was perched on the turtle's head—and saw an arrow scratched on the turtle's back pointing down the narrow street. Modo began walking in that direction, and at the next corner, another pile of turtle rocks pointed down a different path. Modo was surprised to see one of Tommy's favorite rocks was the turtle's head. On the turtle's back was scratched *Get Help*. A block away, Modo found another turtle, again facing in another direction. The message: *Bad Magick*. Modo began to walk faster, following the path of turtles, soon racing from one corner to the next. Each turtle had a message: *Trap, Get Help, Be Careful.* The last turtle's message was *Sorry – T.*

Suddenly Modo stopped. Mercedes flew down and landed on the last rock turtle, looking up at Modo, his head cocked to one side, his shiny black eyes staring at the boy.

"I know, Mercedes, I know. He's at Old Turtle Pond," Modo said quietly. With the wind ruffling his hair and lifting Mercedes's feathers, Modo stood thinking. He could run home and get Dad and Gavin, but that would take time. He could go to the pond and watch and wait. He didn't even know who or what might be at the pond. The bad bigger boys? A Gorling? What? Still, it was Tommy, so he didn't have a choice, did he?

"Mercedes," Modo said, "go get Dad and Gavin. Fly! Now!" Modo ran toward the pond as Mercedes flew into the wind, heading home for help.

Violin and Flute

34

Shouting for Tommy, Modo came skidding to a halt in the muddy leaves at the edge of the water. Suspended in the opening above the old well at the end of the pond, Tommy appeared lifeless, his eyes glazed over, his arms flopping at his side.

"Tommy?" Modo whispered.

"He can't hear you," a woman cackled as she stepped out of the cave, a red cape flying out behind her in the wind. "So, boy, do you remember me?"

"Yes," Modo said. "You sat behind me at the bookstore."

"Good," Warneke said. "You're a smart boy. As you can see, destroying you will not be hard. Let me show you."

The woman walked past the well and stood at the edge of the pond. Her hair seemed to jump off her head in wild windblown corkscrews. Facing into the gale, she lifted a

violin from under her cape, slipped it under her chin, and began to tune the strings. Tommy's arms and legs began twitching, his face changing into a frightening grimace as the sound attacked his body.

Modo moved back away from the pond. The Gorling began to play her violin, a fast shrieking run of notes up and down the scale. What could he do? How could he save Tommy? Be calm, breathe...think.

"The only possible way to defeat a Gorling is through the art form they magickally use."

Modo knew what he had to do.

Reaching behind him, Modo pulled his wooden flute from his back pocket, stepping closer to the pond. When the woman saw the flute, she began to play in a fury.

Higher and higher, faster and faster, the violin screeched and raged long, screaming wails accented with short piercing jabs. No song or melody was recognizable in the playing, just the music of rage as she bowed violently. The sound was as overwhelming as the howling gales of a hurricane. She swayed back and forth, the wind blowing her cape straight out like a flag.

Modo's knees began shaking as he saw Tommy begin to sink down toward the well. Closing his eyes, he began to play, the wind stealing his breath so he had hardly enough to blow through the flute. Modo's music slowly began to soar, rising and falling, filling the spaces between the violin's squeals. He played the music of the trees, the melodies of the birds, the song of the creek, the rhythm of the rocks, all the anthems of Anterg. As he played, his breath steadied, the sound becoming stronger and more even. His fingers seemed to float over the tone holes, dancing to the melodies and rhythms of the tunes. The low tones were full and sonorous, the high tones bright and pure. Modo was thinking *defeat, defeat, defeat.* But the Gorling woman seemed oblivious to his mind talk.

On and on the music battled, the wooden flute constantly returning to attack the violin's vengeance. But Modo was tiring, his fingers moving on their own as Tommy was sinking, his ankles into the well now.

There was only one thing left to do. Modo turned away from the wind, took a deep breath, and began to play "A Dragon's Wish." Over and over he played it, reaching out to Eboo with his mind. He called "Come back, please come back! Eboo, where are you? Come back! Come back!" Modo felt the Call rising on the wind, swirling through the treetops, soaring to the sky.

As the wind blew stronger and harder, the water on the pond began peaking in small white caps, and the evening sky grew darker. With even more determination, the woman played furiously, her fingers a blur as they moved up and down the violin's neck. Her elbow high in the air like the broken wing of an injured bird, the bow flew across the strings shredding the horsehair strands.

Finally, exhausted, Modo was ready to give up. *Now I've failed Tommy too*, he thought.

Sinking to his knees, Modo felt a sudden sense of calm fill him, his heart and mind becoming still. Anterg still.

Closing his eyes again, he began the Call one last time, playing peace into the wind, calling for Eboo. The violin continued to wail, but as Modo became calmer, the wind slowly dropped to a breeze.

Then a rushing sound filled the air like a thousand birds winging through the darkening sky. Eboo was there, but he was not alone flying over the pond. Behind him, eleven red, green, and blue dragons descended slowly as Eboo landed next to Modo.

"Hum the Call, Eboo, hum," Modo whispered.

"We will hum, one and all, but Modo must still play the Call."

Modo began playing, weakly at first. Then Eboo began humming, once again matching Modo's flute note for

note. The humming became louder as it was strengthened by the other dragons. The murmuring covered the pond, vibrating the rocks, shaking the trees.

The violin began to falter, but then the woman pulled herself up straight and launched into another musical attack. Higher still and even faster, the violin yelped and yowled, grated and howled!

"Keep playing, Modo," Father yelled over the shrill assaults and the dragon's drone. "You can do this! We're here to help."

But Father was not alone. Gavin, Orrin, and Jack were there too. As Father began sending sky lanterns up to brighten the growing darkness, Gavin saw Tommy and ran directly to the well, stretched his arms toward the thicket, and began moving his fingers. Instantly, leafy vines and branches shot out and began winding under Tommy's arms, holding him above the dark hole. Father sent more sky lanterns up, his wand smoking with the effort. In the light, Modo saw Orrin run to one side of the pond, pull out his drawing pad, and draw a wall; seconds later, the wall stood by the pond. Over and over Orrin drew the walls until the pond was surrounded by an echo chamber. Before the last wall appeared, Jack jumped into the chamber with Warneke, Tommy, Modo, and the dragons. The humming hit the walls and began bouncing all around them, drowning out the violin. Then Jack began to dance.

Starting with a slow spin, he turned, gaining speed with each rotation, his arms stretched out from his sides like whirling blades. Jack became a blue blur, sending the hum spinning in a roaring tornado around Warneke. The violin screech became a chaos of notes as she dissolved into a red smear, until, in one ear-splitting scream, the violin blew into smithereens. As he fell to the ground exhausted, Modo saw through the settling smoke that the woman was gone.

Modo lay unconscious by the pond. Jack sank to his knees. Tommy, still dazed, was suspended by Gavin's vines above the well. A red cape hung limply from a tree branch. Only the dragons still moved in the lantern light of the chamber.

Atlantica Dragons

35

Father tapped the chamber walls with his wand, and they instantly vanished. Gavin raced to get Tommy out of the vines and safely to the ground. Still dazed, Tommy slumped to his knees. Orrin ran to Jack and helped him up; Jack's head was still clouded with the spinning.

Father picked up Modo, grabbed Warneke's cape, and walked over to Eboo. Orrin, Jack, and Gavin, carrying Tommy, joined him. Together the magicks and natural stood facing the magnificent dragons. Overhead, a few sky lanterns still spread light across the pond. Now that the danger was past, the boys stood in amazement, staring at the dragons.

"We are honored by your presence," Father said, lowering his head slightly. "We are also delighted to know you still live in our world, as you do in our hearts and memories. Thank you for coming."

A red dragon began moving toward Father. Proceeding slowly, the dragon's scarred wings rustled as he walked. Faded patches of gold adorned his red body and tail scales, and one gold band circled his neck. Although his talons were chipped and cracked, he moved with great dignity, his head swaying slowing from side to side with each step. As he drew closer the smell of cinnamon and carnations floated over Father and the boys.

"My name is Calum, and these are my brethren. I am an old dragon, beyond the years of rhyming. The great white dragon, Dreyken, sent us with Eboo to help his young pard and to give them both time to learn. Dreyken wishes Winkleberry to know that he still lives large in Dreyken's heart. We will return to Blooming Grove knowing Anterg is safe for now."

All the dragons, except Eboo, turned toward the pond, preparing to rise up and fly.

"Come, Eboo," Calum called. "It is time."

Father, still holding Modo in his arms, looked at Eboo. His large black eyes staring intently at father, Eboo bowed his head and then spoke:

"Eboo loves Modo, but Eboo must go; we are too young, this he must know. Eboo goes with his brethren to question and grow; to learn how to help our minds meet and flow. Eboo will return when we are ready, until then, you must keep Modo steady."

Shuffling forward, Eboo laid his snout on Modo's shoulder, humming "A Dragon's Wish." A large dragon tear fell on the boy's head.

In the next instant, the sky over the pond was filled with dragons, green wings whooshing, red spiked tails waving, blue snouts sniffing the air. With eyes to the sky, Father and the boys watched the majestic dragons soar over the Blue Mountains, and then they were gone.

"Mr. Malarkey," Orrin said. "Is she dead, is she gone?"

"I don't know, Orrin," Father replied. "We thought she was gone once before."

Above the pond, the last lantern winked out, leaving them in dark shadows.

"Gavin," Father said, "Can you carry Tommy?"

"Yes," Gavin replied. "Dad, is Modo okay?"

"He will be, Mother's a healer. We'll get them all home and she will set them right."

With Mercedes leading the way, the small group moved down the now quiet path back to the village through the cottage-lined walkways. Squirrels, birds, and chipmunks watched silently from the trees and porch roofs, honoring the protectors of Anterg.

An hour later, after Mother had checked them over, Orrin and Jack went home to rest and fill in their parents about what had happened. On their journals, above the oak leaves and acorns, a red half-moon now appeared— the courage moon. The same moon appeared on Gavin's journal. Father left Modo in Mother's care and sent Mercedes with messages for Principal Winkleberry, Tommy's mom, and Dunmore Throop. They all arrived within minutes. Father shared Dreyken's message with Principal Winkleberry, and, also, Eboo's words.

Mother mixed a sweet tea for Tommy. Slowly, sipping his drink, he told the story of Warneke and Julian. Feeling miserable for his part in what happened, he hung his head. Tommy's mom hugged him and quietly cried.

"Here," Gavin said, handing Tommy his journal. "It fell out of your pocket when I got you out of the vines."

"Thanks," Tommy said. "Wait! Look at the cover, there's a blue star. What's a blue star for? I've never seen one before."

"I believe," Father said, "it's a gifting star."

"A gifting star? I don't have any gifts," Tommy protested.

"Actually," Professor Winkleberry said, "I believe you have several gifts. Your rock sculptures are surely one, but I don't believe that's what this star is about."

"Then, what?" Tommy asked, frowning in confusion.

"You possess what is possibly the most powerful and important gift—the gift of true friendship. You were willing to lose everything—your home, your freedom, seeing your mother—to warn your friend. To give him a chance to survive. That will always be the most treasured gift of all! Now, I do believe you also need a courage star!" Professor Winkleberry tapped Tommy's journal with his wand, and immediately a red star appeared next to the blue one. Unexpectedly, a small silver sliver of moon rested between the two stars.

"Why is there a moon on my journal?" Tommy whispered. "I'm a natural."

"It is a sign of the bond between naturals and magicks," Professor Winkleberry replied. "Now finish your tea, my young friend."

"I know it's crazy," Tommy said. "But I hope Julian is all right. Maybe he's free now."

DRAGON PARD

Father stood on the bedroom deck looking out at the sunrise; Mercedes sat on the railing preening his feathers. Anterg was almost still, with a slight breeze from the south. Sunlight was just beginning to penetrate the tree canopy of brightly colored leaves. Off to one side, Dunmore Throop stood holding Warneke's red cape.

"Are you sure she is really gone?" Dunmore asked Father repeatedly.

"I told you," Father replied. "She became a red spinning blur, there was a scream, the violin exploded, and she was gone. You're holding all that was left."

The deck door opened. Gavin stuck his head out and said, "Dad, Modo's waking up, you better come in."

Slowly opening his eyes, Modo realized he was in his parents' bedroom. Finkle was curled up next to him, and Tommy sat at the end of the bed picking loose threads in the quilt. Father came in from the deck, and Gavin and Professor Winkleberry stood by the door. Dunmore Throop remained out on the deck.

Mother brought Modo some lemonade and asked, "How do you feel?"

"Tommy? Is he all right?"

"I'm fine, Modo. I'm sorry, I didn't know what to do."

Modo smiled and nodded. "Thank you for the turtles. Are Jack and Orrin mad that I didn't tell them about Eboo?"

"No," Gavin said. "I think they understood. They were awesome at the pond. They're home sleeping now. Wait until you see the new red moons we all got on our journals! Tommy got two stars and a moon. Really cool! Let's check your journal, Modo. Get it out."

Modo leaned to his side and pulled the journal out of his back pocket. He put on his glasses, squinted his eyes, and looked closely at the cover.

"What's the matter?" Gavin asked. "No red moon?"

"There's nothing at all, not even the oak leaves and acorns or the moon I already had!" Modo exclaimed.

"Let me see," Principal Winkleberry said, taking an old battered journal out of his coat pocket.

With the journals lying side by side, Modo saw the light imprint of a dragon on Principal Winkleberry's book. Everyone watched in amazement as a ghostlike image of the dragon rose off the cover, briefly moved like smoke in a breeze, and hovered over Modo's journal. Slowly sinking down, the dragon became a sharp imprint on Modo's cover. Principal Winkleberry lifted the silver dragon pendant over his head and gently placed it around Modo's neck.

"The sword has been passed," Principal Winkleberry whispered. "Modo, you are now the dragon pard of Anterg."

"The sword, sir?" Modo asked.

"In time, dear boy, in time."

Modo held the silver dragon in his hand, suddenly exhausted. His eyes wanted to close, but he had to know.

"Where's Eboo? Is he back in the cave?"

No one answered. No one moved.

Principal Winkleberry looked down at Modo and smiled. "He's with Dreyken, Modo. You both have some growing up to do, but you know he will return."

Dunmore opened the door to the balcony. "Modo," he said, "come out here—hurry."

Modo got up and shuffled across the room and out onto the balcony, followed by Principal Winkleberry.

"Listen," Dunmore said.

At first Modo wasn't sure what he heard, but he soon smiled as humming floated on the breeze from the Blue Mountains. "A Dragon's Wish" was being added to the Anthem of Anterg.

"I'll be ready, Eboo," Modo whispered. "I'll be ready."